# CALLIE'S TREASURES

## A Search for Authentic Love and Intimacy

*June (JB) Price*

**JB Price**

Copyright © 2014 JB Price.

All rights reserved. No part of this book may be used or reproduced by any means, graphic, electronic, or mechanical, including photocopying, recording, taping or by any information storage retrieval system without the written permission of the publisher except in the case of brief quotations embodied in critical articles and reviews.

Scriptures taken from the Holy Bible, New International Version®, NIV®. Copyright © 1973, 1978, 1984, 2011 by Biblica, Inc.™ Used by permission of Zondervan. All rights reserved worldwide. www.zondervan.com The "NIV" and "New International Version" are trademarks registered in the United States Patent and Trademark Office by Biblica, Inc.™ All rights reserved.

Scripture taken from the *Amplified Bible*, Copyright © 1954, 1958, 1962, 1964, 1965, 1987 by The Lockman Foundation. Used by permission.

Out of respect for the One who is above all others, the author chooses to capitalize all references to the Trinity, including pronouns. That includes any and all names used to describe Him.

This is a work of fiction. All of the characters, names, incidents, organizations, and dialogue in this novel are either the products of the author's imagination or are used fictitiously.

WestBow Press books may be ordered through booksellers or by contacting:

WestBow Press
A Division of Thomas Nelson & Zondervan
1663 Liberty Drive
Bloomington, IN 47403
www.westbowpress.com
1 (866) 928-1240

Because of the dynamic nature of the Internet, any web addresses or links contained in this book may have changed since publication and may no longer be valid. The views expressed in this work are solely those of the author and do not necessarily reflect the views of the publisher, and the publisher hereby disclaims any responsibility for them.

Cover design by Navigation Advertising, Murfreesboro, TN
Art Direction and Photography by Christian Hidalgo
Graphic Design by James Neal

ISBN: 978-1-4908-3268-5 (sc)
ISBN: 978-1-4908-3269-2 (hc)
ISBN: 978-1-4908-3267-8 (e)

Library of Congress Control Number: 2014907174

Printed in the United States of America.

WestBow Press rev. date: 6/13/2014

Foothills of the Blue Ridge Mountains
1972

## 1 Corinthians 13:4-8

Amplified Bible (AMP)

⁴ Love endures long *and* is patient and kind; love never is envious *nor* boils over with jealousy, is not boastful *or* vainglorious, does not display itself haughtily.

⁵ It is not conceited (arrogant and inflated with pride); it is not rude (unmannerly) *and* does not act unbecomingly. Love (God's love in us) does not insist on its own rights *or* its own way, *for* it is not self-seeking; it is not touchy *or* fretful *or* resentful; it takes no account of the evil done to it [it pays no attention to a suffered wrong].

⁶ It does not rejoice at injustice *and* unrighteousness, but rejoices when right *and* truth prevail.

⁷ Love bears up under anything *and* everything that comes, is ever ready to believe the best of every person, its hopes are fadeless under all circumstances, and it endures everything [without weakening].

⁸ Love never fails [never fades out or becomes obsolete or comes to an end].

## Isaiah 45:3

New International Version (NIV)

³ I will give you hidden treasures, riches stored in secret places, so that you may know that I am the Lord, the God of Israel, who summons you by name.

# Dedication

Callie's Treasures is dedicated to the memory of my dad, Jack Boyd, who not only enjoyed bringing smiles to faces and hearts with his humorous stories, but lived one of the most unselfish lives of anyone I've ever personally known. Thanks Dad. Because of you, I've never found it difficult to believe that God loves me. What a gift to give a child! Twelve years and I still miss you.

# Chapter 1

The downturned windows of a new Malibu invited the fresh mountain air and the warmth of a late spring day to fill the car and refresh its passengers. Callie Adams and her family were en route to a nearby farm where a hayride and cookout with friends and family had been planned. Today was her sixteenth birthday.

"Hey, Callie! Ever heard the old saying, 'Sweet sixteen and never been kissed'? Is that you?" inquisitive ten year old Carla asked. Though the sisters shared the same attractive, dark features as their mom, the similarities ended there. Conscientious, thoughtful and people pleasing Callie was often embarrassed by her younger sister's outspoken, unfiltered spontaneity, while fearless and flighty Carla frequently became impatient with Callie's organization and meticulous mind set. Some folks thought Callie a perfectionist. Carla insisted annoying was a better description. She often asked her parents which one of them had been adopted.

"Yeah, it's true, Carla. Maybe that's because I've never had a date." Callie was hopeful that both of those deficits would be eliminated soon, though no one had indicated an interest. And being honest … she couldn't think of anyone she wanted to kiss … yet. "Why did you ask?"

"Oh, some of my friends and I overheard a conversation a few days ago that stirred our curiosity. A group of your male peers were discussing you and your upcoming birthday, and … well … drawing straws. I was just wondering who won."

Callie let that scene sink in. "That's embarrassing! Especially since no one has asked! Maybe there were no short straws … or perhaps the guy who won wasn't interested." That thought was as encouraging as an *unsatisfactory* on a report card.

As their minds were brooding over those possibilities, their eyes were drawn to the blue-green liquid ribbon that meandered through the valley as they neared their destination. Though they had grown up in the foothills bordering the James River, its ever-moving water always summoned them to places and adventures beyond these valleys and surrounding mountains. So far neither had been out of the state of Virginia.

Their parents listened but made no comment. It was a well-known fact that the Adams girls were not allowed to date until they turned sixteen. All four knew that this was a day of new beginnings for Callie -- a rite of passage.

Upon arrival, Callie's parents asked her to remain in the car while they finished some last minute surprise preparations. Carla jumped out to help.

Making sure no one was watching, the lingering tomboy inclination in Callie prompted her to crawl over the bench seat and slide into the driver's spot. She was daydreaming about dating and getting her driver's license when the back door swung open. David Henderson, her cousin, settled on the seat. The farm which was located in Campbell County, Virginia, belonged to his folks, Joseph and Ella. They had graciously offered it for tonight's festivities.

"Hey, Cal! How's the birthday girl?" David scooted to the middle, leaned forward and rested his arms on the back of the front seat.

Last Friday she and her family had attended David's eighteenth birthday and high school graduation celebration. She turned in his direction and realized he was unusually close. She edged closer to the door. "I'm excited, Cousin. I think sixteen is going to be a fabulous year, but I can't wait to be eighteen and out of high school like you."

His proximity and those deep set, dark eyes sparkling with an unfamiliar expression caused her to turn her focus back to the scurry of folks in front of her. Several charcoal grills covered with burgers were giving off smoke signals reminiscent of those who first roamed these hills. While trying to mentally decipher the mysterious vibes David was giving off, she noted that her dad and his were getting the wagon readied for the hayride.

Not only did David have a curious look in his eyes, he was wearing a new cologne. "Fishing for a new girl, Cousin? My nose informs me that you've changed colognes. And not that my opinion matters, but I like this one better."

She glanced in the rearview mirror to catch his reaction. He winked at her and then patted her shoulder. "Wow! I'm impressed and pleased that you noticed. And yes, I definitely have a new girl in mind."

As she turned to meet his gaze, she was reminded that this was the face the local girls declared to be the handsomest in three counties. What girl could resist him? Throw in his charismatic personality and the poor girl wouldn't have a chance. Mulling over her invitation list, she wondered who the lucky friend was.

Trying to clear her head and disrupt his new vibes, she attempted to remember life without him. She couldn't. He was two years older and had taken on the role of her protector years ago. She had always felt comfortable and safe around him. In fact, he was her favorite cousin, although she could never remember how many generations ago the kinship occurred.

His parents were salt-of-the-earth kind of folks. His mom, who had battled breast cancer four years ago, was now coping with recurring malignancy that had spread to other organs. Although she was taking some new experimental treatment, the doctors weren't giving the family much hope. Callie hated that cruel and merciless disease and the devastating impact it was taking on the family. She wondered if that had any bearing on his missing last week's community service project and church social.

"Hey, I didn't see you at the carwash or picnic at Riverside, Saturday. What happened?"

"Dad needed my help at the dealership. His new secretary doesn't know the ropes yet, so they needed help catching up. Nothing like spending a Saturday with your head in a filing cabinet." He inched closer. "What did I miss?"

David found himself adrift in the bottomless depths of Callie's dark chocolate, doe eyes as she related the story of a couple of squirrels that invaded the food stash at the picnic while they were wading in the river. As she turned to watch the events unfolding in front of them, he admired her cameo perfect profile and marveled at the beauty who was maturing before his eyes. From her chestnut brown hair to her sandaled feet, she was becoming one of God's loveliest creatures, though that fact was still camouflaged at times by her tomboyish clothes and ways.

Whether she was unaware of her natural beauty or didn't put much stock in outward appearances, he didn't know, but that attribute made her calm, gentle spirit and fun-loving ways even more appealing. Her genuine love for others and an unusual zest for life predictably drew folks to her … and that included David. What had started as a childish attraction at the old swimming hole years ago had blossomed into a major crush. He wondered if she had ever suspected his interest. He had dated other girls, but none very long. Not one measured up to Callie. He had been patiently waiting for this day.

Her attention had been caught by the noisy group of male peers who were congregating near the barn. "So which one of those guys has claimed you for your first date?"

Callie's cheeks turned a rosy hue, and all traces of humor left her face. "Did you hear about the drawing of straws, too?"

"I don't know anything about drawing straws, but I do know it's time someone took you out. Which one was brave enough to ask? Rob Lincoln has been a secret admirer for over a year, and I recently heard Jason Lankford mention an interest. Just figured one of them had spoken up by now."

Callie chuckled. "Well, Cousin, bravery must be in short supply among the lot of them or else it's just talk, because my phone has been silent and my calendar is still blank."

"Great! Their delay is my opportunity. What would you think of me being your first date?"

It took a few seconds for his words to register and she turned abruptly to look at him. "Are you teasing me, Cousin?"

"No, Cal. I'm serious. We've been best buds for years. Why not give your favorite cousin a chance? I'll take you out to dinner or we could go skating. I hear you've been taking lessons."

Callie glared at him for a few seconds. "You do know that cousins don't date, don't you, David? And last time I checked, we are still related. I think your new cologne is messing with your brain. You've been acting a little strange this evening ... and now this."

He was prepared for her response ... well, at least the cousin part. "Cal, although our families are close, our blood connection is distant at best. That's a moot-point."

She hesitated as though weighing his words and intent, but kept her eyes glued to his. David realized that dampness was forming on his hands and his chest suddenly felt a little tight. He had asked his share of girls for dates and had never been turned down. He was beginning to wonder if the one that mattered the most would be his first rejection. That was something he hadn't prepared for. He began to brace himself.

Before responding, she broke the stare and relaxed some. "Don't get me wrong, David. I think it would be fun to date you, but ..." She broke off and gazed out the side window.

"But what, Callie?"

Shifting yet again in his direction, she spoke with a gentle honesty. "Well ... the truth is ... I've never considered you in a romantic way. You're like an older brother to me. I feel like your sis ..."

He placed a finger against those rose-petal, soft lips before she could finish and lost himself in her trusting, but questioning eyes. He purposely leaned in closer. "I don't want to be your brother, Callie Adams. I want to be your date."

Her jaw dropped and she turned away ... again. "What will folks say?"

"Callie, I've never been one to live my life based on the bias of folks around me and that's been one of the traits I've admired in you." He gave her time to process that statement. "What are you really afraid of? Me?"

He gently placed a hand under her chin and turned her face toward his. Their eyes locked. His brain turned to mush and his heart took over. *Mercy! I want to kiss her more than I want that new car dad has ordered for my graduation gift.*

At that awkward moment, the driver's door flew open and Carla leaned in. "Mom says you can come out now." She cast a snooping glance at the startled twosome. "What is going on between you two?"

Callie expelled a noticeable sigh of relief, slipped out of the car and ignored Carla's interrogation while leaving David alone and his question unanswered.

Recovering quickly from the unexpected interruption, David caught up with Callie before she reached the crowd. He would have his answer. Stepping in front of her and walking backwards got her attention. "Cal, will you ask your folks if it's okay for us to go out Friday? I … uh … I meant what I said."

She stopped and smiled at him with a new shyness as others began to move in their direction. "I will ask."

He relaxed and took a deep breath as he stepped aside for the small mob of folks headed her way. As they surrounded her, he disappeared into the house.

His mother, Ella Henderson, sat in the den on the couch leaning against a pile of pillows. David knew that folks would routinely cycle in and out to visit and check on her, and yet it pained him to see her too weak to socialize outdoors with the others.

"Did you ask her?" Ella had guessed David's feelings for Callie more than two years ago and had been the first to encourage him to follow his heart. Though they were distant cousins, she and Joseph already considered Callie family.

"She was shocked, Mom, but finally agreed to ask Uncle John and Aunt Beth."

"Then all is as it should be." She gently squeezed his hand and turned to watch the party unfolding on the lawn.

David noted her fatigue and knew she needed to rest. He kissed her on the cheek and headed out as Dorothy Jenkins, a close friend and neighbor, entered to sit with her. She would be sensitive and let her rest.

He left feeling the growing pain of slowly losing his mom. She was the warmth, the balance, and the heart of their home. She let David and

Joseph know up front that God was in control of life and death and she was trusting Him. David recalled his mom's words to his dad the first time David witnessed Joseph weeping openly. "Joseph, we have loved each other since we climbed trees together as children. When I married you, I never expected you to fix all of life's hurts. Though you can't remove my pain, you are loving me through it … just as you promised. That's all you can do, Love."

David had seriously considered and even discussed postponing his schooling, but neither would allow it. They wanted him to move on with his life, find a good girl -- both hoped it would be Callie – and eventually settle down in business with his dad. They had already told him that the house would be transferred to him on his wedding day. His parents' hopes to fill the house with little Hendersons had been denied. They were delighted that he had caught their vision of a large family living within its walls. They knew that being an only child could be lonely and challenging at times. And this was such a time.

Sometime tonight David planned to ask Callie to visit with his mom tomorrow afternoon. He wanted his two favorite girls to spend as much time together as possible. Reflecting on Callie's love for this place and his folks' love for her put a smile on his face.

He stood on the porch and searched for the birthday girl. A tinge of jealously stirred when he observed his friend, Rob Lincoln, enjoying her company. *Too late, old buddy. She's spoken for.* As if she knew he was watching, she lifted her eyes towards the house and waved. With the slightest of motions she beckoned him to join them. His feet willingly complied. Catching her eyes as he joined the crowd, he realized she was inviting him to be with her tonight as more than a cousin. He wanted to click his heels. He knew where he would be sitting on the hayride … and whose hand would be tucked in his.

# Chapter 2

The morning after the party Callie slipped into her chair at the breakfast table, grateful that Carla had chosen to spend the night at a friend's house. It was the perfect time to discuss David's surprising conversation and question.

As she contemplated her own new dating interest, she recalled tales of her mom and dad's whirlwind romance. John had accepted a teaching position in one of the local schools, fell in love with the younger teacher in the next classroom and three months later convinced her to change her last name to his. While Beth tells of being drawn to his maturity and captured by his romantic ways, John admits he was smitten by her charm and beauty from the start.

John was now the principal of a local elementary school and Beth had been a stay at home mom since Callie joined the family. Even after eighteen years of marriage their love was strong ... and evident. Callie realized that she wanted to experience that kind of love and marriage someday. That thought took her back to last night ... and David.

"Did you enjoy your party last night, Callie?" Mom was putting breakfast on the table.

"It was the most exciting night of my life, Mom. Thanks to you two."

"Was that because you turned sixteen or because a certain young man finally admitted his interest in you?" Dad asked with this face glued to the newspaper.

Callie's jaw dropped and Mom chimed in. "Don't pick on her, John. We want her to talk to us. Not clam up in embarrassment."

Dad laid the paper on the table and apologized before commenting that he was glad David Henderson was to be her first date. Besides being distant relatives and family friends, Dad had been David's Little League baseball coach for three years. He supposed aloud that David could be counted on to behave himself.

"How did you know he asked me?" Callie was baffled by her dad's knowledge of David's interest.

"David apparently had a moment of guilt after he popped the question to you first. He talked to me shortly before we left. That boy's had a crush on you for years."

If the warmth of her cheeks was any indication, Callie knew her blush would make Maybelline jealous. She wasn't sure how she felt about her Dad's news flash but was certain this was neither the time nor place to analyze or discuss it. She elected to move to David's other request. "I noticed Aunt Ella seemed more tired than usual last night. Uncle Joseph helped her to her room before I could break away to say hello. David asked me to stop by for a visit this afternoon. Dad, would you mind dropping me off after lunch? David said he would bring me home."

Mom and Dad gave each other a knowing look that made Callie wonder if Carla had blabbered about the awkward moment in the car. "Sure, Honey. I can do that."

John did drop Callie off at the entrance to Henderson Hills later that afternoon. As she watched his car disappear around the bend and began to walk up the drive, she had the surreal feeling of walking onto the canvas of a breathtaking masterpiece. The splendor of these majestic peaks and valleys teaming with hints and clues of their Designer always captivated her mind and soothed her soul.

The Henderson house and other structures, which had been built with their surroundings and location in mind, reflected a beautiful blend of the creation of God and the genius of those made in His image. Callie imagined this place could have been next door to Eden. After savoring the awe this setting radiated, she pushed the doorbell and listened as the chimes announced her arrival.

Joseph welcomed her with his usual charm and enthusiasm. After a few moments of polite small talk, he disappeared to make certain that Ella was ready. Callie was left sitting in the guest parlor of the beautiful, spacious country home.

Ella's knack for design and gift of hospitality ensured that few felt anything but comfortable from the minute they stepped inside though it was one of the finest homes in the county. And should guests wander across the parlor to view the Henderson's stables and a sizeable barn tucked behind a row of trees, their thoughts would be drawn to the Creator of the beauty surrounding them, rather than the assets needed to maintain it.

Callie considered Joseph and Ella as she wandered through the parlor, looking at photographs and smiling at the impressive antiques tastefully placed throughout the room. *Aunt Ella is a treasure,* Callie reflected. Her adherence to and blending of the code of etiquette of the Old South with a genuine love for people reminded Callie of the virtuous woman pictured in Proverbs 31.

In his mid-forties, tall and handsome Joseph Henderson with his trademark mustache and curly black hair, was one of the most respected men in Campbell County. He could have held a political office like his father, but he preferred a quieter life. He owned the largest auto dealership in the area and although the workmanship and ingenuity of the automobile intrigued him, he was quick to admit that a ride on one of his sought-after Tennessee Walking horses delighted him more. The cars were his livelihood. The horses ... his love. Some he sold to finance his hobby, but the others were given to camps and ranches where they served children and adults with special needs. Callie noted traits of Joseph repeated in his son.

A unique picture frame hanging on the wall always captured Callie's attention. Under the glass, three perfect ribbon bows were pressed -- one blue and two pink. Callie knew they were a memorial to David's three siblings who had each passed away shortly before birth. Some things in life are impossible to understand. In Callie's mind this rambling house begged for the large family they had been denied.

"She's ready, Callie," Joseph said, interrupting her thoughts. "You'll find her in the upstairs family room."

Callie found her resting on a lounger. It was heartbreaking to know that while Ella had survived a previous bout with cancer several years ago, she was having to face the disease a second time. The poor woman was so thin and sallow that it hurt to look at her.

"Don't look so sad, sweet Callie." Aunt Ella's shrinking frame was covered with a beautiful afghan Beth had made for her. "My days were recorded before I drew a breath and I am concentrating on living, not dying."

Callie smiled at this statement since Aunt Ella said it often -- in good health and ill -- to express her generally sunny outlook towards life. If it was raining, she saw it as a good day to curl up with a great book. If a plan was canceled, she took it as an opportunity to make a new one. If the worst happened, Aunt Ella allowed it to serve as a reminder to thank God in all things -- no matter how difficult those things might be. To her ... every day was a gift.

"I'm so glad to see you, Aunt Ella," Callie said as she took a seat beside her. As is the custom in many southern families, when folks are unusually close, they encourage their children to address the adults as *uncle* or *aunt*. Callie had called Joseph and Ella uncle and aunt all her life though the connection was actually distant cousin.

Ella thanked her for coming and motioned to a plate of tasty desserts sitting on a tray with a glass of homemade iced tea. She encouraged Callie to enjoy the treats. Callie did as requested, trying not to show her dismay when Ella ate none. Mom had explained her cousin and friend was slowly losing her appetite.

The two chatted about family happenings and local events until Ella finally pinned Callie with a teasing smile. "Do you not have some personal news to share, Dear?"

"I do, but I suspect you already know that David asked me for a date Friday night. I don't think it's a big deal."

Ella opened her mouth to reply, then paused at the sound of approaching footsteps. "Callie, that comment hurts my feelings. No big deal, huh?" David teased as he entered the room.

Callie turned to see him leaning against the door jam and was surprised by the little hitch in her breathing. The handsome face she had known all of her life was smiling at her as if he had won a sweepstakes … and she was the prize. "I think you should give me a chance before you declare me 'no big deal', Cal. One date can open the door to all kinds of possibilities."

"That's true, Son, so don't give her reason to change her mind." Ella's tongue-in-cheek comment warmed Callie's heart.

"I certainly don't want that to happen." He shifted his gaze to his mother. "Mom, I know it's time for you to rest, so with your permission I'll gladly entertain your guest."

That comment put a playful smile on his mom's face. "I can see that will not be an unpleasant task." Turning her attention to her young visitor, she laid her hand on Callie's arm. "Thank you so much for coming to see me, Callie. You know you are welcome in this house anytime."

Callie kissed her cheek and turned to leave the room. "Come back soon, Callie, and let me know what kind of date my son turns out to be."

"You can count on it, Aunt Ella." She had been contemplating the same question herself.

Callie followed David down the front staircase and politely declined his offer to go horseback riding before he took her home.

"You know, Callie, it would help my ego if you showed a smidgeon of interest in me as your date."

Callie eyeballed him as she placed her hands on her hips. "Hey, Cousin, I'm not only new to the dating scene, but my brain is struggling to switch you from cousin to dating status. Your ego will just have to suffer while I make the needed adjustments. I just never thought of you *that* way."

Suddenly playful, he cocked his head to the side and raised an eyebrow. "I wish you'd quit calling me *cousin*. And what way, Callie?"

"You know …" She wouldn't have to worry about wearing rouge if she kept blushing around him all the time.

"Yes, I do, and I hope you don't wrestle with the changes too long."

She bit her lip in sudden shyness and tried to turn away, but he caught her hand and settled it in the crook of his arm. Smiling at her with his confident, familiar smile, he marched her outdoors where he helped her into the car. Callie felt her heart do a somersault.

# Chapter 3

David was uncommonly jittery by the time he pulled into the Adams' driveway Friday evening. The uneasiness escalated as he approached the door. *What is the deal? I've known this family all my life.* Before he could reason out the answer, John opened the door and invited him in. Conversation had always flowed easily between them, but this evening it was more guarded. John and David were keenly aware that tonight's event was bringing a different dynamic to their relationship.

They talked about the local happenings of the week and then John looked at the young man who had been a few months old when he moved to this town almost eighteen years ago. "You know she's my princess, David. I'm trusting you to always keep that in mind."

"You can count on it, Uncle John."

"Since you are dating my daughter, let's drop the *uncle* handle. Just call me John."

"I'll have to work on that, Sir."

Sensing David's unusual edginess, John was endeavoring to bring some levity into the mix when Callie and Beth walked into the room. David jumped to his feet as an internal *wow* robbed him of his breath. The delightful tomboy cousin had been replaced by a stunning, decidedly feminine date. Though appropriately dressed for skating, she was definitely all girl. Her usually pony-tailed, dark chestnut, full-bodied hair was loose … and inviting. A hint of makeup accentuated her already dazzling eyes -- which were reflecting the same nervous excitement he was experiencing. "You look … uh … really nice, Cal."

"You don't look too bad yourself, Cousin -- oh, I mean, David." That slip of the tongue broke through the awkwardness of the moment. "What can I say? Old habits are hard to break. Last week you were my cousin and this week you are my date." Callie laughed and the others joined in.

When John moved to open the door for them, David followed his lead by clasping Callie's hand and assuring her parents that he would have her home by 11 o'clock. Callie had already apprised them of their activities for the evening.

Some of the strain between them evaporated as they walked to the car -- minus an audience of two hovering parents. After assisting Callie into the passenger seat, he leaned in. "We're going to work on the cousin label tonight, Cal. It has to go. And get this. Your dad asked me to drop the uncle label and just call him John."

As he was backing out the drive, she began to softly chant. "David, not cousin. David, not cousin. David, not cousin." She looked at him and smiled. "Be patient ... Cousin."

"Try this one. Sweetheart, not cousin. Sweetheart, not cousin."

True to her quick to listen but slow to speak nature, she was quiet for the next few miles. He knew she was processing both his words and their implications.

"David, are you joshing me with all your serious comments? I don't know how to respond when you say those things."

They had reached the skating rink. After he turned off the engine, he reached for her hand. "Let's talk a few minutes before we head in. Okay?"

She nodded.

"Callie, I've had a crush on you for years and last weekend at your birthday party, my heart took the final plunge. I not only want to be your first date. I want to be your only date ... from here on out. I'm trusting that in time your heart will catch up with mine." Her look of disbelief alerted him that he was getting too serious too fast, but he was opting for honesty up front.

She sat quietly for several minutes before responding. "You need to remember I'm at the bottom of the learning curve in matters of the heart." She hesitated. "But who knows? Given time I might like you better as a boyfriend."

"Oh, sweet Callie, I'm counting on that." *I've got to change directions. I'm wanting to trade in that car for a kiss again.* "Now let's go have some fun. Since you've been taking skating lessons, you can be my instructor tonight ... if you promise not to mock me. This tall body on wheels is a close imitation of a giraffe on ice. You have your work cut out for you."

Callie laughed. "Giraffe on ice? You can't be *that* awkward."

"You think not? We'll pick up that thought in about thirty minutes."

David had hoped to stay close since this was their first time together as a couple, but he had a slight problem. Callie was grace on wheels while he gave new meaning to graceless and redefined floor time. Callie watched with amused wonder and after fifteen minutes took pity on the skating casualty. "Giraffe on ice comes pretty close. How can you be so smooth and coordinated on the basketball court and shockingly clumsy here?"

"Hey, those eight, undersized, round, ever-moving appendages drain every ounce of balance, coordination and confidence out of my body, Callie. Why do you think I've never showed up for skating socials?"

"You just need some tips and lots of practice. Come, skate with me. Maybe I can help."

Callie reached for his hand and to his delight, that small act of kindness -- or maybe it was pity -- helped. Her skill and knowledge were the shots in the arm he had needed. She took it in stride when he caused both of them to crash a couple of times, but little by little his confidence grew and as he began to relax, his balance improved. A couple of hours of instruction and practice convinced Callie they could participate in the couples skating. He was doubtful but she had been such a good sport that he couldn't say no. And they did ... rather clumsily. David told her they were making memories ... the kind you share with your children and grandchildren.

"Yeah, a giraffe on skates does make a rather interesting story, but I think the gangly creature has left the rink ... though there were moments I had my doubts. I'd hang onto that basketball scholarship if I were you. I don't think your future is at the skating rink."

"Thanks for that vote of confidence, Girlfriend. My aching body needs a break and I'm desperate for a drink. Want one?" She nodded and took off skating … solo.

The next time David spotted Callie, he almost lost his balance. It was a good thing her drink was in a bottle. She was skate dancing with a familiar looking partner and they had the floor all to themselves. The lights were low and everyone else, mesmerized by the stirring depiction of dual grace in motion, had backed up to the rails. He was fascinated by their precision, beauty of form, singleness of execution and interpretation of the music. Unexpectedly, a bolt of jealously shot through him. That familiar face belonged to Cliff Wilson, the owner's son. *When did Casanova get back in town and why is my date his partner?*

When the music ended, Callie pointed towards David. Cliff let go of her hand as they skated his way. David set her drink on the nearest table and contemplated inviting Cliff to take a walk … but considering he still had skates on, he opted for being nice. *Stay calm, Henderson. Be very wise.* He put on his best smile and reached out a hand.

"Hi, Cliff. When did you get back in town? See you've met my date." He reached for Callie's hand and drew her close.

"Hi, Dave. Last week. Dad has asked me to take over the rink and that includes all classes and private lessons. Yeah, your date not only grew up while I was gone, she has become one of the best skaters Mack and this rink have produced. Dad had told me about her. I couldn't resist asking for a chance to skate with her tonight when I saw her on the floor alone. Hope you didn't mind."

"Nah, I'm sure Callie enjoyed a partner who can actually skate. The two of you turned it into art. That was beautiful."

"It's easy with the right partner," Cliff said winking at Callie. Without giving David a chance to respond further, he focused on Callie. "Thanks, Cal. See you next week." The cad deliberately checked out the scenery and skated away.

Callie reached for her drink and quenched the thirst the last two plus hours had created. "Aren't you thirsty, David?"

Ignoring her question, he asked his own. "Callie, I had no idea you could skate like that. Are your lessons weekly?"

"You are not the only one with a secret or two, David Henderson," Callie teased as she playfully bumped his arm. "And if you don't quit staring at me like that, I'm going to call you *cousin* the rest of the night."

"That would not be appropriate. I promise you that I am not having cousin thoughts at this moment." *Cliff is now her skating instructor. This is not good news.* "You didn't answer my question."

"Yes, they are weekly. And in case you are wondering … Cliff used that same song for our first skate dancing class."

"Isn't that interesting?" *Don't go there Henderson, not now.* "Hey, if we're going to get a sundae before I have to take you home, we'd better be on our way. Have you had enough for one night?"

"That sounds delicious. And I've had an unforgettable night. I can't remember the last time I've laughed so much."

"You be kind, Girlfriend. Your fun was at the expense of my pride and bruised body. Let's ditch these wheels for tonight."

As they walked to the car, he pulled her into his space. "Callie, I've been wanting to hug you all evening but the giraffe in me knew better than to try. Would you mind?"

She grinned sheepishly, gave him a quick cousin hug and stepped back.

His lop-sided grin spoke louder than his words. "That wasn't exactly what I had in mind."

Her eyebrows shot up as she scrutinized all six foot three inches of him. "Oh."

His hands moved up her arms pulling her closer and then enclosed her in a tender embrace. This was definitely not a *cousin* hug. She looked up. "I don't think I'll be calling you *cousin* anymore."

"One hug cured that? Wow!" The urge to kiss her was strong again. "We'd better break this up before we get other ideas." He leaned down, brushed her forehead with a gentle kiss and opened her door.

David had dated other girls. Never had he experienced the emotions, the excitement, the fun, the laughter, the sensations or the jealously this beautiful one had released in him tonight. In his heart she was already his *forever girl*. He was still processing his thoughts regarding Cliff. He had to be at least twenty-two. That was too old for Callie. Wasn't it? Maybe he'd look Cliff up next week ... and catch up.

Before leaving her that night, he lined up a date for next weekend. Resisting the urge to kiss her, he settled for another light kiss on her forehead as he bid her goodnight.

They spent the summer transitioning from cousins to sweethearts. The only sadness was Ella's failing health. She had stopped all treatments declaring that David and Callie were better medicine than anything the doctor was giving her. None of them talked much about it, but they knew they were losing her. She tolerated no sad, gloomy talk or faces. Beth was helping with her care now. David and Callie spent much of their time together at the Hendersons. He was grateful for the attachment between Callie and his mom.

About a week before he had to leave for the University of Virginia, Callie stopped by for a visit. As soon as she entered her room, Ella asked her to walk down to the river to check on David. "We had a little talk earlier in the day and I saw him head that way afterwards. That's been several hours. I'm concerned about him, Callie. Will you find him for me?"

"Sure." As Callie turned to leave, Ella spoke again. "He's going to need you in the coming days and weeks, Callie. Other than his dad he has no one else who understands his grief. I know my time for leaving is soon. Stay close, Sweet Girl. Help him be strong and encourage him to trust the Lord through it all, will you?"

With tears rolling down her cheeks, Callie turned back to one of the bravest ladies she knew and kissed her cheek. "I'll be here, Aunt Ella. I'm rather fond of your son."

Ella reached out to hug her. "You'll never know the gift you've been to me, Callie. I love you, daughter of my heart. Now go find our boy."

As Callie neared one of their favorite fishing spots, she saw him pacing back and forth along the riverbank. She quietly edged closer and heard him begging God for his mother's life. Witnessing his pain and recalling Ella's emaciated body caused her to question the goodness of God for a moment. None of this looked or felt like love.

She stepped into his line of vision. As though a life line had been thrown to him, his tormented expression softened, and he moved in her direction. She felt the weight of his pain as he embraced her and wept. Her tears and pleas joined his. "Thanks for coming, Callie."

"Your mom sent me."

"She called me into her room today. She was basically telling me goodbye. With every word she uttered ... with every promise I made, I felt like my heart and hers were being ripped piece by piece from our bodies. I wondered how either of us continued to breathe.

"Callie, what are we going to do without her? I hear Dad downstairs at all hours of the night weeping and praying. We put on our smiles, but inside a part of us is dying with her. She is so brave and confident of God's will in all of this, and I want to scream that a loving God would not allow something this horrible to happen to someone He loves. I don't have her faith, Callie, and right now, I'm not sure how I feel about God."

He reached for her hand and suggested they sit. Without awareness, as was often the case, the wonder and tranquility of the creation that surrounded them were working their way into their questioning minds and aching hearts.

"David, I don't know the answers to your doubts and questions, but I do believe that the God who carved out this river and formed these mountains is big enough to handle them. I don't think He's put off by your honesty or doubts. Can you trust Him even though nothing makes sense at the moment?"

He lifted her chin so that she was close enough to feel his breath. "I choose to trust and you are a major reason. Callie, if I didn't have you during this time, I don't know how I would handle Mom's illness and approaching death. This love I have for you must have its roots in God. It's a connection I can't explain and God uses that and you to comfort me in the midst of all this. Thank you for being you and for being here with me."

He kept her close. "David, do you think we should head back to the house? Your mom sent me to check on you. She's concerned."

He nodded. As Callie turned to face him, their eyes met. He had kept her at arms' length all summer but no longer. He tenderly kissed the girl who had invaded his heart and was sharing his grief. Though it wasn't an overly passionate kiss, still it was their first.

David rose and helped her up. "Let's check on Mom and then saddle a couple of horses and check out the north trail."

Hand in hand they walked back to his house to check on Ella before enjoying one of their favorite ways to spend time together ... horseback riding along the James River and trails of the Blue Ridge foothills.

# Chapter 4

The summer had ended and David's studies at the University of Virginia, known as UV by those attending, had beckoned. Adjusting to life away from home, including the pressures of being a student athlete and coping with Ella's merciless disease and her imminent death were hard enough. But leaving behind the only person who came close to understanding the internal havoc all of this was having on him made this the most testing time of his life -- so far.

He went home as many weekends as possible before the official basketball season opened. Ella died sixteen days before his first collegiate basketball game. Unreal would best explain the five days that followed for David.

He kept Callie close as much as possible. They took walks in the woods and rode horses through the fields. She listened as he unloaded his anger over the injustice of his mom's last year of life and early death and his growing questions and struggles with the goodness of God for a faithful daughter. Out of the darkness, David could see one ray of sunshine ... Callie. And he gravitated to her like a moth to a flame.

David and Joseph talked. David wanted to drop out of school for the year, work with his dad and start over next year. Forfeiting his basketball scholarship would be small potatoes compared to the immeasurable loss of his mother. "David, your mother would be very disappointed if you didn't return to school. We'll make it -- one day at a time -- with God's help and the support of our friends. Folks who have walked this path warn against making important decisions in the midst of grief. I'm asking you to return to school."

Reluctantly, David complied and headed back to UV knowing that one of the two most influential persons in his life was gone and that void could never be filled again. Due to basketball practices and games, home visits were curtailed which allowed him to live in intermittent denial. If he didn't go home, he didn't have to face a house or life without her.

In Lynchburg, Callie was pouring her extra time and energy into earning an academic scholarship. The bright spot was Joseph's decision to attend David's home basketball games and include her and John on the weekends. The sixty-nine mile excursion proved to be therapeutic for all of them.

Four weeks later, the semester ended and David was on his way to the Adams' place to pick up Callie.

As Callie was slipping into her dress, Carla entered her room. "You look terrific, Sis. Want me to clip a sprig of mistletoe in your hair?"

"Don't you think that's a little too obvious, Carla?"

"Well, don't you want him to kiss you?"

"Yes, but hopefully it won't require mistletoe." The sound of an approaching vehicle alerted them that her date had arrived.

By the time David knocked, Carla was at the door. In a voice too low for anyone else to hear, she informed him of the location of the mistletoe. "Just in case you need any help."

He winked at her. "Thanks. I'll remember that."

He was exchanging greetings with John and Beth when Callie walked in. The attraction between them was like opposite poles of magnets. "Hi, Cal."

She blushed as Carla's nudges caused her to stumble into his arms. "Sorry about that," Callie offered.

Carla reached around Callie, punched David's arm and pointed at the mistletoe. "Ah, come on. We all know you want to kiss her."

David leaned close and lightly kissed Callie on the cheek. "How's that, Cousin Carla?"

"Pretty disappointing, but I guess it'll have to do." She huffed and headed upstairs.

Still holding Callie's hand, David moved toward the door. "Guess we'd better run if we're going to meet Dad. I'm taking her to the house tonight, but Dad will be there. Is that okay?"

"Sure, Son. Callie explained your plans and reasons. We understand your reluctance to go home alone."

After enjoying dinner with Joseph, all three headed to Henderson Hills. David was understandably quiet. By the time he parked, tears were trailing down his cheeks. "Callie, I've loved this place as long as I can remember and I still do, but I'd gladly give it all away to have Mom back." The reservoir of pent-up grief ruptured. David laid his head on the steering wheel as the raw reality of losing his mom washed over him.

"I've been trying to label this unknown shadow that has become my companion. Now I know. It's Loss. Not just the empty house tonight but all the empty places in all my tomorrows. There's a void in me … a hole that no one else can ever fill, Callie."

As they entered the motherless house, years of memories crowded his mind and stirred his emotions.

Tears were plentiful that night for all three. Joseph reminded David of the three Henderson children who were with their mother now. Picturing his mom with them brought a measure of peace.

Beth had helped Joseph turn a portion of the parlor into *Ella's corner*. The threesome spent most of their time there, not only mourning her loss, but celebrating her life as they perused old photo albums. It had been a difficult homecoming and a different date.

"Mom's sickness and death have been part of our dating lives from the beginning, Callie. Tonight reminded me of Mom's admonition to live life to the fullest. I can't bring her back, but I can honor her wishes. Would you rather go skating or hone our archery skills tomorrow?"

"Let's skate. We need to laugh," Callie teased.

"Yeah, and we need to talk about your skating lessons."

"I don't take lessons anymore, David. I talked to Mom and Dad and we all decided it would be best if I quit."

"Mind telling me why?"

"I was beginning to feel uncomfortable with Cliff as my instructor."

"If he tried anything with you, Cal, so help me …"

"That's why I didn't tell you. You had enough on your mind."

He pulled her into his arms and waited for her eyes to meet his. "Callie Adams, I've been looking out for you about as long as you've been in the world and now that you are my girl, I take it personally when anyone is disrespectful. Was he?"

"He was getting a little too friendly during our lessons. I stopped it before anything happened, David. Please don't say anything. I think he got the message."

"Well, in case he didn't, he and I will have a chat. I'm glad you told your mom and dad, Cal, but promise me that you'll let me know if any of the boys around here give you any trouble."

"Okay, I promise."

Their ride home was quiet as both were reflecting on the events of the evening.

He didn't need the mistletoe to kiss his girl. He smiled as the moving curtain at the younger sister's bedroom window indicated she now knew that, too.

Their days together were sweet. At times memories of his mom hit without warning but he was taking his dad's advice. One day at a time. Having Callie in his life helped.

# Chapter 5

Joseph continued to attend all home games while Callie and John joined him for those scheduled on the weekends. David looked forward to his cheerleaders' attendance and the morsels of time they had together. He not only played harder when they were present, but seeing and being with Callie was a tonic to his lethargic soul.

One night after a game, David's roommate, Jake Roberts, asked if the girl with his dad was a sister or his girlfriend. "That's Callie, Jake. She's more than a girlfriend. I plan to marry her one day."

"Man, I was hoping for a sister. She is some babe. I know you've been struggling with the loss of your mom. I'm glad you have a girl like that to help you cope."

"Jake, it's true Callie is helping me cope with losing Mom, but not in the way you are talking about."

"Henderson, surely you don't adhere to that archaic rubbish about saving sex for marriage." He turned and faced David. "You do, don't you? That's why you never join in our conversations! You've never been with a woman, have you?"

David didn't respond but was very aware that his blush left no doubt.

"Roomie, you are out of touch with the times. There's nothing like a night with a beautiful, willing female to help you forget your troubles. I'll bet Josie would be interested. I think she has a crush on you."

David had encountered Jake's younger sister the times Jake invited him to join the family for Sunday dinner. They lived in a classy section of town called Rugby Heights. David knew that trying to change Jake's mind was as futile as trying to change the direction of the wind. Only God could do either. He dropped the conversation and refused to comment any time Jake brought it up. Thankfully Josie was still in high school and David could limit his contact with her. She did occasionally show up at the dorm, and he had to admit she was a work of art. He admired the view, but didn't linger.

Basketball season ended and the remaining weekends were spent at home. He breathed easier, grateful that he had survived the first year of college and the loss of his mother. His eighteenth year had been challenging.

# Chapter 6

Summer came and David plunged into his continuing apprenticeship with his dad. Callie had been hired as a gofer for the local newspaper. She was considering a career in journalism and knew this job could confirm or negate that possibility.

Ella had been gone seven months and the Henderson men continued to deal with that reality. Neither wanted to eat out all the time, so Joseph casually suggested they invite Callie to join them at least once a week for a cooking project. The suggestion quickly turned into a weekly culinary adventure. The threesome relished their successes and suffered good-naturedly through their less than appetizing failures. Tuesday evenings they could be found at the Adams' table enjoying Beth's home cooking and seeking cooking tips for their next gourmet undertaking.

At least two Saturday mornings of every month the Adams girls helped out in the Henderson stables. The Henderson and Adams families were growing closer -- like Callie and David.

As their affection for each other grew, so did their physical attraction. David talked to his dad and shared Jake's comments.

"God's wisdom surpasses ours, David. Sex was and is His idea. He pronounced it good within the boundaries He established. He admonishes us to avoid even a hint of immorality. Though those limitations feel restrictive and seem archaic at times, they provide guidelines for love, sex, marriage and intimacy that house some of life's most intimate pleasures and personal joys. Ignoring them opens the doors to many of life's deepest wounds and greatest tragedies."

Joseph looked at his son and wondered what else Ella would have shared. "You and Callie need to openly discuss these issues. The culture will bombard you with contradictions. Your own flesh will protest. Decide now that God is wiser than you and until you do understand His reasons, choose to obey. You'll find the strength to obey comes from a personal relationship with God. Don't ignore that part of your life now that you are away from home."

"Dad, do you struggle with being tempted now that Mom is gone?"

"I'm still grieving the loss of your mom, David, but I'm not unaware of an attractive woman. Of course, I'm tempted. But being older and having experienced the blessings and beauty of God's protective guidelines in marriage makes resisting easier than when I was your age. I well remember those days. They were challenging. Flee temptations, Son. Being tempted is not a sin. Yielding is."

The next time Callie and David were together he brought up the subject of sex and God's guidelines. They were honest and admitted the need for boundaries and agreed to revisit the issue from time to time. Though challenging and no longer popular, they chose to trust God's wisdom.

David and Callie's relationship continued to mature the summer of 1973 which made parting harder.

# CHAPTER 7

David's first day back on campus as a sophomore hinted of challenging changes. Jake's sister, Josie, was now a freshman ... living on campus. Being Jake's roommate made it impossible to completely avoid the sexy temptress. Her clothes were as provocative as her speech was suggestive. It was evident that she was aware of her assets and confident of their impact on the male species. She was finding creative ways to invade David's private space. He had never dealt with anyone as blatant ... or as alluring.

He managed fairly well until official basketball season brought a halt to his weekends at Henderson Hills. His dad's attendance at all home games and Callie's presence for those on the weekends were not only welcomed, but crucial for David's sanity and chastity, although he kept praying that the Lynchburg cheering section didn't run into Jake's family.

Seeing Callie for even a short period of time gave him the courage to resist and flee his would-be seducer. He was ashamed to tell anyone that thoughts of Josie were beginning to linger after an encounter or conversation. He kept trying to control his thoughts and run when tempted. Neither seemed as easy to put into practice as those teaching about them claimed. The rest of school was going well, but this new challenge was beginning to create a major disturbance. Coping with Josie made the semester feel more like an endurance test than an educational endeavor.

Though the Christmas break was short, David welcomed the breather. He and Callie had five wonderful days before he had to leave for scheduled holiday games and a second semester of dealing with *Delilah*. He was developing new insight into Joseph's and Samson's dilemmas.

Optimism had him hoping for a reprieve the second semester. Josie shot that down fast. Her mindset had not changed. On the first road trip of the New Year, David engaged Jake about an issue that had agitated him since Josie's arrival. "I can understand why living on campus is a perk for you, especially during basketball season, but why did Josie choose campus housing when your home is so close?"

"Mom and Dad allowed her to make that decision. She said she needed to experience life away from home. Is she getting to you, Roomie?"

"No, just wondering." And he let that conversation die.

Josie dated others but never slowed her pursuit of David. Little by little she kept making new inroads into his mind and guilt was growing along with lustful thoughts. The scattered games that brought Callie to the campus weren't enough to protect his thought life from the sexual harassment Josie was throwing his way. He panicked when she invaded his dreams. *Is there something wrong with me? The thoughts and desires she stirs make me feel dirty and a betrayer of Callie. How am I supposed to deal with this?*

That realization planted a seed-thought which began taking root deep inside. He had been praying for escape routes and strength, but what he really needed was a change.

His most recent phone conversation with Callie strengthened his new resolve and confirmed his new direction. She had accepted an academic scholarship to the University of Oklahoma -- over a thousand miles away. *What is she thinking? That means we won't see each other at all during the semesters. She is the only reason I make trips home before and after basketball season and her weekend trips here for ballgames have given me reason to stand strong ... well, at least I'm trying. How can I handle Josie if Callie is not in my life?*

He called his dad the next day to discuss his idea. Joseph listened as David talked about his struggles of being single, in love with one girl about to move over a thousand miles away and being pursued by a mini-skirted, free-love advocate daily. Joseph agreed the plan could work, but he had reservations about Callie buying into it. He had been the airport taxi for the Adams' trip to the University of Oklahoma and knew the level of excitement they were experiencing. That information didn't change David's mind. He felt there was no other possibility, at least none that didn't generate fear in his heart and mind.

Joseph was kind but honest. "Son, lust is not your root problem, though I know it feels that way right now. When lust or any sin is winning, it indicates a lacking in your personal relationship with God."

"Dad, what I need is a change. I need to get *Delilah* out of my life and Callie in. We need to get married. She can transfer here. She'll understand. She has to."

"For your sake, I hope you're right, but don't get your hopes up."

# Chapter 8

Callie's high school graduation was scheduled for the day after David got home for the summer. That gave him one day to purchase a special ring and plan his strategy. If they were going to have a late summer wedding, he had no time to waste. He decided to pop the question after her graduation celebration.

Soon after arriving home, he shared his ideas with Joseph. "Give me a few minutes, Son, I have something for you."

After depositing his suitcases in his room, David walked to Ella's corner. Looking at all the keepsakes brought tears to his eyes. *I miss you, Mom. I sure could use your wisdom ... and prayers.*

Joseph returned and before sitting down, handed him a rather old-looking, black velvet ring box. "Open it, David."

As David stared at his mom's engagement and wedding rings, Joseph explained, "Ella wanted Callie to have these when you decided it was time. She said this way she would always be part of your lives."

A warm blanket of love encircled him as tears of loss made paths down his cheeks. David thanked his dad ... and missed his mom.

All through her graduation ceremony, David kept patting the outside of his pocket to be sure the ring box was still there. He was as nervous as a young coon dog on his first hunt. *What if she says no? What if ...?* He quickly aborted those thoughts.

After graduation, Callie rode with David to the community center where her folks were hosting a barbeque starting at noon. Square dancing and free instructions for those interested would follow. Ordinarily, he enjoyed these social gatherings but he wasn't looking forward to this one. *Surely folks won't stay till dark.*

Callie noticed his uneasiness. "David, are you okay?"

"Okay? Well, let's see. I'm home for the summer. My girlfriend, who graduated from high school today and will turn eighteen next week, keeps redefining beautiful. Sweetheart, I'm more than okay. I'm excited."

She scooted across the bench seat, looped her left arm through his right and stayed close the rest of the trip while they caught up on current happenings.

Contemplating the possibility that she could soon be his wife sent his thoughts in one direction and then realistically acknowledging that she could say no sent them in another. Come to think of it -- he did feel a little queasy. He would be relieved when they could talk.

Like the evening of her sixteenth birthday, he had to share her while she graciously mingled with those who came on her behalf. Her fashionable, soft, off-white dress showcased her dark features and grown-up figure. *Lord, she is so incredibly beautiful -- inside and out. I dream of a life with her and can't imagine one without her.*

He managed to grab her for a couple of dances. "Callie, I've been homesick for you this last semester. Our brief visits kept me going, but also made me aware that I don't like being away from you. Hope you don't think I'm being selfish, but I'm looking forward to these folks leaving so I can have you to myself."

"I've missed you, too. You keep talking like that and I'm going to kiss you right here in front of God and the world." David stopped when her dark chocolate eyes focused at his lips. He couldn't resist. Before she could object, he kissed her.

Applause and whistles reminded them they weren't alone. Half embarrassed and half teasing, he cast a glance at Rob Lincoln, "Just wanted to remind a couple of my friends which way the wind is blowing." Playfully, Rob snatched her away and David good-naturedly went back to watching and socializing. He wasn't dancing with anyone else. He only had one girl on his mind -- his!

As David feared, folks were in no hurry to leave as the first sizable gathering of spring, tasty southern food, down home music and a chance to sharpen their dancing skills for free bid them linger. Between the Dalton Bros. Barbeque and the Blue Ridge Mountain Boys' music, it was a deliciously entertaining affair.

Too many hours later a few folks finally began to trickle out the door. The nervous boyfriend breathed a sigh of relief when Callie changed into jeans as he had requested. With their parents' knowledge and permission, the twosome headed to the Henderson farm for a horseback ride. God and nature were cooperating with his plans. It was going to be a perfect afternoon and evening.

They saddled a couple of horses and headed to their favorite spot, the swimming and fishing hole his father had carved into some of the bottom land from a branch off the James River. He led. She followed.

David helped her dismount and arranged for the horses to graze. He unrolled an old quilt, placed it on the ground and invited her to join him. He could not wait any longer. "We need to talk, Callie."

She seemed uneasy all of a sudden. "Okay, David. I'm listening."

"Do you remember your sixteenth birthday?"

She visibly relaxed. "Oh … I remember. That's the night my favorite cousin asked me for a date."

"And now two years later, how do you feel about your *favorite* cousin?"

"Hmm," she hesitated as though in deep thought. "Well, I'd say he was Prince Charming in disguise."

"Prince Charming, huh?" He reached into his pocket and pulled out the old ring box.

As he opened it, Callie gasped aloud as both hands met over her heart. "Oh, David! Your mother's ring!" Tears began to form.

"I was just as surprised as you when Dad gave it to me. This is Mom's way of being part of our lives, Callie."

"That blows me away, David. I can't imagine wearing her ring."

"Well, Sweetheart, I'm going to try to change your mind about that. I had this prepared speech about God going back to his original design for women when he formed you, Cal, but the simple truth is that I love you and want to spend the rest of my life loving and being loved by you. I know you love me, but do you love me enough to marry me?"

The shock of the proposal and Ella's ring had evidently rendered her mute. He removed the ring and reached for her left hand. Still she didn't move or speak. Her eyes were glued on his mom's antique diamond and ruby ring.

"You are scaring me, Callie. My nerves are already shot, my stomach has forgotten how to digest food and now it seems my heart has joined the mutiny. Have mercy on me, Woman."

The stare was broken and the tears began to trickle down her cheeks as she looked into his eyes. Rising on both knees, he leaned in and gently wiped her tears. "Hey, Sweetheart, I've got my neck and our future on the line. Will you let me put this ring on your finger?"

She smiled through her tears and nodded.

A sense of calm began to settle over his frazzled nerves. "I'm sorry, Cal. I didn't hear you. What did you say?"

Forcing the words through her paralyzed vocal cords made her sound like someone who had just finished a marathon. She uttered a breathy, "Y-e-s."

He slipped the ring on her finger and clutched her in a hug that almost suffocated her. "Hey ... if you don't loosen up ... your already stunned bride-to-be is going to faint before you kiss her."

He loosened his hold and studied the face of the girl who was going to be his bride. His lips caressed hers and deepened as she responded warmly. Then gently, she began to pull away. "David, we aren't married yet, so maybe we should postpone these bedroom kisses. The warning bells are ringing. I have to admit I'm tempted, but we made a promise to God and each other ... to wait."

He groaned and eased back nodding in agreement. "I know, Callie." He took a couple of deep breaths. "Besides, I have another question."

He settled back down on the quilt. "I promise I'll behave. There's something else we need to talk about. Please hear me out. Okay?"

"You mean there's more to this mind-blowing day! I thought graduation and the celebration were terrific and then you spring the proposal and your mom's ring on me. I don't think you can surpass those events, but give it a try. I'm all ears."

No beating around the bush for David. "I want to get married this summer before we head back to school."

She was startled ... again. "Whoa! That trumped them all!"

She started to say more but he put a finger to her lips. "Just listen. This is not a sudden decision, Callie. Two years of college life and being away from you have taken a toll on me. I live with guys who think we are fools to abstain from sex until marriage and brag about their exploits and conquests on a regular basis. I'm surrounded by girls with too much flesh showing who have bought into the same lie.

"I love and want only you. You've already figured out that the longer we date the stronger my attraction to you becomes. Paul said it is better to marry than burn with passion. I'd say burning with passion describes my situation rather well, so I decided to adhere to his wisdom. Long term dating and engagements make it tough to deal with sexual boundaries. I am ready for all that marriage offers, Callie."

She shot him a questioning look.

He continued. "I know that you would have to forfeit your scholarship and transfer to UV. I've talked to dad and he agrees it is doable. I'll take care of the finances and see that your school bills get paid.

"I'm aware this plan has drawbacks. We are young to be marrying with so much schooling in front of us, but the possibilities that lie ahead if we don't, outweigh all downsides in my mind. Please consider it! You don't have to answer me this minute, but we need to make a decision soon."

The air stilled between them. Her swarm of butterflies had been scattered by an invading herd of wild horses. Eighteen years had not prepared her for the myriad of thoughts, the mix of raw emotions or enticing possibilities that were propelling her through the highs and lows of such a decision. If she was hearing correctly, and at this point she wasn't sure, the urgency centered on the sexual issues. Should sexual needs and desires be the driving force behind the timing of a marriage? Well, Paul seemed to be on his side. She knew David had put much thought into this request. He did not make hasty or rash decisions.

"David, about the time I think life with you has settled, you surprise me with another one of your mind blowing moments. You've set world records today.

"So much is going through my mind. I'm ready to commit to marrying you. And there is a part of me that wants to shout a loud *YES* even now to marrying this summer, but there's another part that questions the timing and whether the sexual issue should be the predominant reason. I'm not sure I'm ready to marry in the next ten weeks. Give me a week … one week from today I'll have my answer for you. Is that okay?"

David reached for her closest hand and breathed easier than he had in days. "That's more than okay. I was petrified that you would say no right off. At least you are willing to think about it. And it's not just about sex, Callie. Granted I'd love to wake up to you every morning, but I want to share all of my life with you, in and out of the bedroom."

He helped her to her feet and pulled her into a warm embrace. Callie pushed back some. "David, it seems the last two years away have been harder on you than you've indicated … until now."

"The first year wasn't that hard, but the last one has been difficult in this area. The moral upheaval of the 60's is fermenting on college campuses, Callie. In and out of the classroom. And this is not just about me. You are heading to a secular college where you will be faced with the same changing moral code. Sweetheart, you are going to be temptation to some of those admiring males and I'm willing to bet a few of them are going to turn your head. You've never dated anyone but me. My concern is not just for me. It's for you and us, as well."

"Hey, this is not a ring to be ignored," she interjected. "I'll just flash it around for those who have problems listening. I think I should be the one concerned. What alerts the girls around you that you are engaged? You are a handsome, young athlete who oozes southern charm. I know there are girls in your path who find you as appealing and desirable as I do. Maybe I need to buy you an engagement ring."

"Appealing and desirable? You've never told me that before, Callie. I had hoped, but it's good to hear."

"Give me a break, David Henderson. Our boundaries keep me from expressing everything I feel for you, but don't ever doubt that my hormones are healthy and in constant need of reminders concerning you and us."

"Yeah? Well, there are girls out there who don't live by your boundaries and I don't want to have to deal them and their hormones anymore, Callie. I want to be with you and love you. That would greatly reduce the impact of my temptations."

"Give me time and space, David. A week ... with no contact. I don't want to be pressured. Okay?"

"No way! You *cannot* be serious! I give you an engagement ring and you tell me to hit the road? I arrived home yesterday after being away for months. Didn't you miss me, Callie?" And before she could answer, he added, "Does this shut-out include church? And what about your birthday?"

She cuffed his shoulder playfully and moved toward the horses. "I think I can handle being with you during services and this ring covers my birthday as far as I'm concerned." She planted a light kiss on his cheek.

He resembled a little boy whose puppy had rejected him for his best friend.

"I do love you, Prince Charming, and want to do what's best for both of us."

His smile fused with an impish expression as he helped her mount her horse. "Hey, when does the no-touch, no-see, no-speak fast begin?" He hesitated only a second and looked up. "Are you sure I can't stop by in the evenings? I promise not to say a word. We could just sit on the porch swing and cuddle a while."

"Don't you dare! I need to make this decision with a clear head and your cuddles leads to kisses which muddle my brain."

That remark produced a huge smile and a low murmur. "Brain muddler, huh?" He mounted and indicated that she should lead the way. There was little conversation between them. Each was lost in their own labyrinth of thoughts and emotions ... and possibilities.

After they had unsaddled the horses, Callie stopped under a light to take a closer look at her ring. It was exquisite. David walked up behind her, put his arms around her and took her ring hand in his. "Do you like it?" Turning in his arms to face him she confessed, "I've always admired it and am finding it hard to believe that it's now on my finger. It looks old."

He pulled her closer. "It belonged to Mom's grandmother. Tradition has been to give it to the oldest granddaughter, but since Mom wasn't going to live to see hers, she decided you should have it."

She tiptoed to kiss him and whispered. "I'll treasure it, David, but not as much as I cherish you and your family." And kiss him she did. Warning bells pealed and lights flashed! Was it going to be like this every time they were together? Both voluntarily heeded the warning and walked back to his car.

They spent the rest of the evening with her family. John and Beth were stunned that she was wearing Ella's ring but pleased about the engagement. Carla was being the typical twelve year old sister -- fawning over the ring and David. Callie allowed her to slip it on her finger for a few precious minutes. David stayed as late as the curfew allowed. The fast started tomorrow, except for church services. What a day it had been!

# Chapter 9

David met Callie as she exited the family car Sunday. "Wait up a minute, Cal. Your outlawed boyfriend has something for you."

She smiled ... as glad to see him as he was her. Her parents and Carla moved on ahead to give them privacy.

"Since I'm banned from your life, I decided to give you your birthday present today. Close your eyes." David pulled a white gold chain with an interlocking double heart pendant out of a small white box and fastened it around her neck. "Happy Birthday, my non-cuddled, kissed or muddled, Fiancée."

Callie smiled as she lifted the pendant and took in its imagery. "It's beautiful, David. Thank you." She tiptoed and brushed his cheek with a light kiss.

"Do you understand that my heart is yours, Callie? Regardless of your decision?"

"Yes. And mine belongs to you, David. The necklace says it well."

He reached for her hand as they entered the sanctuary. Heads turned. Evidently Carla had been the harbinger. Congratulations were plentiful. They had a sweet morning together, and to Callie's surprise, David went his way without a fuss.

When David had not shown up by mid-afternoon, the family questioned. When Callie explained, Carla erupted. "Callie, I think it's cruel and mean to accept David's ring and then refuse any type of contact with him. He's been away for the better part of a year."

"Carla, I have one week to make one of the most crucial decisions of my life and my heart gets in the way of my head when I'm around David. He wants to get married this summer. I don't think I'm ready."

"Not ready? Aunt Ella's ring. Uncle Joseph's approval. Mom and Dad's approval. What else is there to think about?"

"Much, Carla ... much."

"I think David Henderson is the dreamiest man in the whole wide world. I know a dozen girls who would jump at the invitation he's handed you. I sure wouldn't have to think twice if I were in your shoes."

"Well, he didn't ask you or any of them." She picked up her tablet to make some more notes and then looked back at Carla. "You wouldn't have a small crush on my fiancée, would you, *little S*ister?"

"You and your lists. You ever think of doing anything spontaneously? Would it be a sin to follow your heart instead of your head ... just once? And I wished you'd quit calling me your *little* sister." With that Carla stomped out of the room leaving Callie with her notebook of pros and cons.

After a week of consideration and discussion with her parents, Callie had reached her decision. She called David at noon Friday and made plans to meet him at his place that evening.

He was waiting for her when she arrived. "I'm serving you notice. There'll be no more of this don't talk, don't touch, don't see fasting between us." Without warning, he hugged her and claimed her lips as if determined to make up for the week apart. "I've missed you, Callie."

"Be still my heart! If it makes you feel any better, Carla gave me so much grief over the shut out that I began to think you two were in cahoots." She stopped and looked at him. "You're weren't, were you?"

His imitation of Rhett Butler's roguish smile and swagger made her laugh. "No, but now that you mention it, Sweetheart. She could be a powerful ally."

She grabbed his hand and started walking towards the porch swing. She could not allow him to muddle her brain before she gave him her answer.

After they settled on the swing, he pulled her close. "It would make me feel somewhat compensated if you confessed to missing me half as much as I've missed you the last six days."

Their faces were so close she got lost in his dark, inviting eyes. She lightly kissed his cheek. He turned the other one and pointed. She laughed. "You are one clueless male! Missed you? I'm willing to wager that my missing was equal to yours, not half. Appealing? Desirable? Healthy hormones? Remember?"

"Really?" His eyes lit up. "I think the pastor may have the afternoon open if you decide to move up the wedding date."

"Not so fast, Romeo. Juliet has reached a decision. Want to hear it?"

He nodded.

"Please let me finish before you comment."

Disappointment spread over his face as he guessed her answer before she said another word.

"David, I'm confident you are the man I want to marry, but I'm only eighteen. I know several of our classmates have married out of high school, but I want more."

Pain squeezed her own heart as she thought of his. "I could give you a list of reasons but the bottom line is -- I'm simply not ready for marriage. If that's a deal breaker with the engagement, I'll understand. Four years is certainly longer than you had in mind when you gave me the ring."

He offered no response, but rose and turned to face the stables. A couple of the horses in the corral looked his way.

Callie continued. "I studied that passage about burning and marrying. It's rather blunt. It agrees with you that it's better to marry than burn with passion, but the verse before it states the reason ... the inability to control your desires and passions. David, are you telling me that is your situation? I thought we were handling the physical temptations in our relationship rather well. Am I wrong?"

He turned and held her gaze. "Callie, it's not us. I've tried to tell you that life at UV is taxing. I'm at my wit's end on the issue. That's why I suggested marriage this summer. Perhaps I'm being selfish in my request." He turned away from her and walked toward the horses.

Watching David struggling with her decision was painful. She knew he would be disappointed but she didn't expect him to be upset or hurt. He was both. *Am I the one being selfish?*

The silent strain developing between them alarmed her. She joined him at the fence but kept quiet. Finally he faced her with an expression of bewilderment. "Callie, I thought God had given me the answer to a serious challenge in my life and now I find it is not going to work out. I have no idea where to go from here." He stepped close enough to clutch one of her hands and led her to her car. "I love you, but now I'm the one who needs time. I know you'll understand." Without another word, he opened her door, kissed her lightly and walked away.

Callie drove home questioning her decision. She was troubled by his response.

# Chapter 10

Week two of the summer vacation passed and still Callie had no word from David. *For crying out loud! Enough is enough. After all, we are engaged -- at least I think we are. There has to be some resolution to our differences.*

She called his house Saturday afternoon. Joseph suggested she drop in.

When Callie arrived, his dad hugged her and pointed to their workout room. David was punishing his body with bench presses. Getting a glimpse into his misery unnerved her. She slowly moved into his line of vision. When their eyes met, his sadness and pain hit her full force. She reached out to him.

"I'm sweaty and stinky, Callie. Let me go shower and then we can talk. I'll meet you at the gazebo." He left to clean up and she headed outside, uneasy with the tension between them.

Soon he joined her with tall glasses of sweet iced tea. Setting the glasses on a bench, he reached for her hands. "I'm glad you came, Callie."

This was not her cheerful David. His somberness triggered a thought. With a twinkle in her eyes, she stated quite seriously. "I thought maybe we could skip the talking for a while and just cuddle and smooch."

His winsome smile broke through and he kissed her softly. Then touching his forehead to hers he confessed. "Callie, this love I have for you frightens me at times. Saying I love you is too simplistic. My love for you is complex and encompassing. I think losing mom plays into it though I can't explain how. When we are apart, there's a void in me. The thought of a thousand miles separating us the next four years almost paralyzes me. If I seem to cling too tightly or move too fast, I'm sorry. I want to live loving you every day ... not just in words but in the fullest expression of my love. Kissing you reminds me of all that I long for and can't have right now, so maybe I need to practice more restraint in that area and believe me ... that will not be easy.

"I spent some time talking with Pastor Walker this week. I shared my desire to marry this summer and your reservations. He helped me come to terms with your decision to wait, but if you change your mind, he and I are ready to proceed ... anytime."

"My heart belongs to you, David. A thousand miles won't change that." She paused and moved to the edge of the porch that offered an awe-inspiring view only God could create. Both were quiet for several minutes and then she turned to face him. "What if we get married after you graduate? That cuts the four years in half. And do you want the ring back for a while?"

He pulled her into a warm embrace. "No, Sweetheart, the ring belongs on your finger. One day you will be my bride. I just have to deal with life until then. And your willingness to give up two years of your hard earned scholarship is noted. It's a fair compromise. Let's go exercise a couple of the horses for a few hours. I don't want to waste anymore of our time together this summer."

They headed for the stables. "You're not upset with me?"

"No, Callie. I'm disappointed but not upset. You've been honest and fair. We are two people in love with two different thoughts about the timing for marrying. This melancholy will give way to the pleasure and joy of living each day to its fullest ... starting now. Mom taught me that."

And with that they saddled two eager horses and spent the rest of the day enjoying the beauty of the place they called home. With two tough engaged weeks behind them, they were determined to make the best of those that were left. And they did. They had a bonding summer. David refused to think about what potentially awaited him in the fall. After all, Josie could develop a new interest by then.

# Chapter 11

Callie had to report to the University of Oklahoma, in Norman, a week earlier than David was scheduled to begin his junior year at UV. Her folks were driving her out. For all holiday and summer breaks, she would be flying out of the Will Rogers Airport in Oklahoma City to Roanoke Regional. The trip was simply too long for an eighteen year old to make unaccompanied.

Although she was excited about this new adventure in her life, her heart was torn over leaving not just family and all she had ever known, but also David -- no, especially David.

It was their last night together before eleven hundred miles would separate them. "David, there have been times when I have wished I had agreed to marry this summer and this is another one."

"Honey, watching you pack and preparing to put all those miles between us is part of the reality I dreaded." He held her close and showered her with lingering kisses. Tears began to trail down her cheeks.

"David, promise you'll call when you can." Her lips found their way instinctively to his as she kissed him with more passion than she had dared to this point. Without another word, she ran into the house.

When she didn't hear him drive away, she pulled back her curtain. He was sitting in his vehicle with his head on the steering wheel. That imagine lingered long after he left.

On a beautiful September morning in 1974, the Adams family began their life changing excursion. Traveling from Virginia through the expanse of Tennessee, across Arkansas into Oklahoma would give them time to reflect on the past and the changes and challenges of the present.

With every mile that registered on the odometer, Callie could feel an inner tug of war between all she had ever known and a future calling her name. She touched the necklace and looked at her ring. There was no going back. She changed her focus.

She had researched the University of Oklahoma during the summer months and shared some interesting facts with the family. "For your information, the university was founded in 1890, seventeen years before Oklahoma became a state. The unique architectural style of the buildings has been tagged Cherokee Gothic because of the influence the Native American tribes of Oklahoma had on the designs. Its library is on the National Registry of Historic Buildings. And get this. More than sixty native tribes still live in Oklahoma. That's more than any other state." Her family was impressed and asked lots of questions. Most she knew. The others she promised to research.

Since OU freshman were required to live on campus, her residential assignment had been determined by the university housing department. Callie's roommate had already moved in when they arrived. John and Beth liked her immediately.

Heather Williamson was also a freshman and her home was only two hours away in Wichita Falls, Texas. Her parents were OU graduates. Meeting her eased some of her parents' concerns about Callie's housing arrangement.

As Callie watched her mom and dad drive away, the meaning of the word, *alone*, became her reality. In a matter of minutes she was separated from everyone from her past and knew no one in her present, except her new roommate of four hours. She fingered her ring, turned and walked into her new world.

Callie and Heather soon realized the godsend that a compatible roommate brings to the college experience. Being freshmen on academic scholarships created a mutual respect and fostered the ideal atmosphere for serious pursuit of their studies while nurturing a growing friendship. They shared enough in common to be comfortable and had enough differences to make life interesting.

Class selections went well for Callie. She was leaning towards a journalism major with a minor in the emerging field of criminal justice. Investigative journalism intrigued her.

To her dad's delight, the Sooners football team was a strong contender for the national title. She knew that would be a topic of conversation when he called.

David called a week after she got settled. Hearing his voice stirred all her feelings for him and she was more aware of the repercussions her personal decision was having on both of them.

By her second week Callie was aware she needed to find a place of Christian fellowship. There were some notices posted in the student union building. She tried several before finding a good fit. She knew this would be her main source for making friends.

A couple of her male counterparts in the group expressed some personal interest early. Callie was upfront about her engagement and they backed off. The ring and necklace were constant reminders of her love and commitment to David. She sometimes wondered what reminded him of his love for her. That thought gave her an idea for David's Christmas gift.

She stayed busy with her studies, got caught up in the hype of Sooners football and enjoyed making new friends. Missing David was now an accepted part of her life. His calls were bittersweet. So she opted for overly busy to compensate.

# Chapter 12

Eleven hundred miles east, any hopes David had that his situation might change were soon crushed. Assertive Josie was still his quandary and she was temptation with a capital T. Other than Callie, she was the most physically attractive woman he'd ever seen. Her long, bouncy, naturally blonde hair, stunning blue eyes and perfect hour glass figure always left a string of males appreciating God's creation. He could have been one of those who admired and walked away, except she kept inviting him to partake. She renewed that offer early this year. He knew she was forbidden fruit, but her image and those invitations were beginning to make him wonder what the fruit might taste like. When he told her of his engagement to Callie, she just smiled. "She's there and we are here, David. If she's so in love with you, why all the miles between you?"

That question had crossed his mind a few dozen times lately. Callie's refusal to marry was one thing, but to choose a school so far away ...

He didn't go home on the weekends anymore. Mom and Callie weren't there, but Josie was definitely here. And she was becoming salve for his wounded ego and company for his lonely heart. Her attention and presence didn't exasperate him as it had in the past. He began to relax and in doing so found her company enjoyable. In addition to a keen sense of humor that made him laugh often, she had a razor sharp mind. As the friendship grew, he reminded her of his engagement and told her that friendship was the extent of their relationship. She grinned.

Thoughts of Callie didn't consume him until he called her or she wrote, so he cut back on the calls. She was the one who said no to the marriage and made the decision to move so far away. He was making the best of it.

The next time Jake invited him to spend time at his folks' place, he went. Of course, Josie showed up. Now that they were comfortable being together, she had added some physical horse play that was tantalizing, but he wasn't letting it get out of control.

Knowing his dad would be attending home games again, David informed Josie of the ground rules. "If you ever make a move to introduce yourself to my dad, I'll be out of your life so fast that all you'll see is my dust. Do you understand me?"

"Don't fret so, David. I've worked too hard to lose you now. I'm ready for the next level of our relationship. You want it, too, but you're still hung up on a girl who cares more about what she wants than what you need. I intend to make you forget her and then you'll be glad to introduce me to your dad. I'll wait."

Although they never officially dated that semester, they were together so much that other students considered them a couple. He knew his mind and emotions were being compromised. Although he admitted to himself that he was having an emotional affair with Josie, he was pleased that he had avoided an actual bedroom scene, even though his mind had traveled that road.

David's trip home was miserable. He could not shut out the memories of his compromising semester with Josie. He felt certain that none of this would have happened if he and Callie were married or if she would have enrolled at UV or even the local college back home. Facing her was going to be tough. He had not called lately.

Since David didn't offer to meet her plane, Callie called him as soon as she got home. Reluctantly, he headed to 612 Overlook Drive. As he pulled in their driveway, he saw her standing outside the front door dressed in a new ski jacket and a matching cap which called attention to her picture perfect face and stunning eyes. All the memories and promises that had been buried beneath his semester of self-indulgence broke through his fabrications and re-ignited his love for her. *God, she is everything I want and need ... but can't have right now. If she only wanted me as much as Josie does.*

She met him as he opened his door. Pushing his guilt aside, he pulled her into his arms and drank in the sweet essence that was Callie. *She is wearing my ring ... my mom's ring! How could I have betrayed her?* And with that thought his guilt became conviction. *I don't deserve her or her love, but I desperately need her. Lord, help me!*

Callie pulled away and studied his face. "David, is something wrong? You haven't called lately and our last two conversations were short and strained. Are we okay?"

Though it was cold and they needed to get inside, he lingered. He wanted to tell her everything. He wanted to unload the guilt and shame he had accumulated. He needed to confess his resentment, but his pride wouldn't let him.

Reaching for her again, he held her loosely. "Yes, something is wrong. My girl is too far away and I'm lonely for her. Callie, I miss you so much that I'm miserable. Even if we weren't married, you could have enrolled at UV. I guess I don't understand why you chose to go to OU."

She stepped out of his embrace. "Because they offered me the best scholarship, David. Is that why you are upset with me?"

He encased her cold hands with his warm ones. "I don't know how to describe all I'm dealing with right now, Callie, but certainly part of it is the distance that you've chosen to put between us. It makes me question the depth of your love for me. Do you not miss me like I miss you? Do you not want to be with me, Callie?"

She dropped his hands and leaned against his car while looking off in the distance. "When I signed with OU, I wasn't wearing your ring, David. We had had no serious talks of marriage and I didn't dream you'd want to marry before you finished school. And to a young girl who's never been out of the state of Virginia, Oklahoma sounded like a neat adventure at the time. I never dreamed that it would cause problems between us. Hindsight always offers the best view."

Facing him again with a sadness of her own, she confessed. "Now I wish I had pursued a scholarship at UV, but I didn't. I can't ask my parents to pay tuition there when I have a full scholarships at OU. It's not what I want, but it's what I have."

She turned her back to hide the tears. "And not miss you? Not want you?"

As he moved behind her and enclosed her in his arms, she leaned her head against his chest and tears flowed. "I stayed busy and worked hard, but missing you never went away. There's an empty place in me without you. And wanting you? It wouldn't be safe to talk about how much I miss or want you, David Henderson."

That revelation and her tears tugged at his heart. "Turn around, Callie. Please." She did. "I'd gladly put everything else in my life on hold and marry you tomorrow if you'd agree." He brushed her tears away and cupping her face with his hands, softly kissed her cheeks, her eyes, and then her lips ... savoring the sweetness and honesty of his girl.

"No fair! You know how to put pressure on a girl, don't you? Today I wish I had Carla's temperament, because right now I can't think of anything I want more. But you know me. I'm too practical to do something rash."

"But you *want* to?"

She nodded and his heart leaped. "That confession will get me through the next semester, Callie." Their lips met again and David was reminded of the difference between his girl and the one whose definition of love was lust. Lust ... he had some of that to deal with.

A day he had dreaded turned out to be sweet and restorative. Callie was more open about her feelings and love for him. She did want and need him. That was emotional and mental adrenaline for David. The next morning he took his favorite horse on a long trail ride and had a long overdue heart to heart talk with God. A time of confession and repentance. A much needed inner cleansing of his soul.

By Christmas their relationship had been fully restored. Christmas caroling with friends for a local nursing home and taking an assignment as Salvation Army bell ringers for an afternoon helped keep the spotlight on the reason for the season.

They exchanged their personal gifts privately. David gave Callie a bottle of Shalini, his favorite perfume. "This scent and you were made for each other. Remember me when you wear it."

"Wow! That is one of my favorites. Thank you."

Her gift for him was a sterling ID bracelet with *David and Callie* engraved on the front and the date of their engagement on the back. She closed the clasp for him. "I have all these beautiful reminders of you, David. I wanted to give you something to remind you of my love for you."

"It's a perfect gift!" He was hoping it would not only be a reminder to him, but a stop sign for Josie.

Their few days together were prized. For David, it had been a time of realigning his heart with God and reaffirming of his love for Callie. Though sad to leave her, his attitude had changed. Callie knew the air had cleared between them. That made parting easier.

Scheduled holiday games called him away early. Having a better understanding of the void that the miles and months would produce, both were determined to be wiser this coming semester. Staying in touch better would help.

The road games gave him time to get his personal game plan in order. He knew things had to change between him and Josie.

When school got under way, it was apparent that Josie had made the same decision ... except her change was in the other direction. She was pulling out all the stops.

Much to her surprise, David laid his new direction on the line. He spoke honestly about his love for Callie, apologized for his behavior last semester and politely informed her that they would never be more than casual friends. He immediately put some boundaries back in place. By studying in the library more and socializing less, he cut out much contact. Avoiding the usual hangouts and declining invitations to Jake's folks further emphasized his determination and new direction. Except for the unavoidable times when she showed up in their dorm room, he did well. If he was alone when she showed up, he immediately left. He wasn't rude, but he was determined. Callie's bracelet was his constant reminder and encourager.

In addition to avoiding Josie when possible, David called Callie at least once each week, sometimes more. She wrote him weekly. The contact kept both on track that semester and triggered anticipation about the summer ahead.

# CHAPTER 13

By the middle of May of 1975, David had finished his junior year and Delta Airlines just delivered his girl who had completed her freshman year. His heart quickened at the sight of her as he was reminded that she was worth waiting for. Her smile and kiss assured him they had three wonderful months ahead.

The first Sunday morning's lesson was taken from I Corinthians 15:33. *Do not be so deceived and misled! Evil companionships corrupt good manners and morals and character.* Life had affirmed that truth and David listened with understanding.

On the work front, Joseph expressed excitement regarding David's aptitude for business and evidence that his studies were beginning to pay off in the work place. Plans to make him a partner were falling in place.

David approached Callie again about a late summer wedding. She asked for one more year at OU but left the final decision to him. He could not and would not ask her to marry him until she had no reservations. Though he was disappointed, he wasn't upset with her this time. They selected July 16, 1976, as their wedding day. They purchased a wedding planner guide and spent much of their time together making plans for their special day next year.

Their summer was filled with work and fun. Their problem had never been finding things to do, but deciding which one. Their mutual love for the outdoors determined many of their choices. The only complaint either had about the summer was its brevity. All too soon, it was time to say goodbye. Nine more months of separation. "Summer was too short, David, but think about it. This time next year we'll be married. You know I don't want to leave you, don't you?"

"Then don't, Callie. Say the word and we'll get married this week. You know I'm ready."

"You are temptation, David Henderson."

He held her close. "Marry me. School can wait."

"It's too late, David. Where would we live? What about school? How would we make it without jobs? Nine more months. Surely we can wait nine more months."

"Callie, don't ever let concern over finances determine your decision about us. That's my department and I'll always provide for you. You got that?"

She nodded. "I know you will. Give me this year, David, and I'll marry you next summer without any reservations."

"I'll call often and you keep those smile-producing and heart-warming letters coming." David stayed as late as her folks would allow that night and was there early the next morning to drive her to the airport. Kidnapping her and taking her to the Justice of the Peace crossed his mind. He wished he had when it came time for her to board the plane. Her tears confirmed what he suspected last night. She would have at least transferred to UV if he had been assertive, but he understood how she felt about her scholarship. She had worked hard for it. He was honoring that.

Parting was, indeed, sweet sorrow.

# Chapter 14

David returned to school for his senior year determined to live honestly before God and with others, especially Josie. His summer had been redemptive and he had no intention of repeating his past mistakes.

For starters, he felt certain his Virginia Cavaliers basketball team had real possibilities this year. Their coach of three years had convinced them that they now had the horses not only to play well, but win big. Good recruitment the last few years had given them the depth they had lacked and Jake had turned into one of the best go-to guys in the ACC. He probably had a career waiting in the NBA. David purposed to be the best he could be on and off the court. He did love the game and the challenges of team play.

Then there was Josie. Thankfully she was dating other guys, but wasn't shy about letting him know she was still interested in and available to him. He kept his boundaries and determination in place.

Out on the plains of Oklahoma, Callie and Heather were roommates by choice this time. What a difference a year makes. They weren't the new kids on the block anymore. It was a more relaxed beginning in one regard but missing David was more pronounced. Letter number one went out the first week and he had already called to check on her.

Callie only had one concern this semester -- biology. She had struggled with all that kingdom, phylum, class, order and family stuff in high school. She dreaded the college level. Her concerns escalated the first day of class when the teacher assigned a football jock named Jesse Collins as her lab partner. She remembered hearing his name some last year as a promising freshman wide receiver, but she had never seen him this close. He certainly wasn't deficient in the looks department, but how would he deal with all those osmosis and diffusion experiments?

From his manly neck to his broad shoulders, on down his tall, muscular body to the penny loafers on his feet, he was a picture of every girl's dream. She had purposely avoided concentrating on his face ... because ... well ... she had a problem with it.

It! Was! Gorgeous! She wanted to stare. Oh, dear, she was! Deep set arctic blue eyes, a face chiseled by God Himself, short, curly, sun-bleached blonde hair and a summer tan that showcased a beautiful set of pearly whites offset by dimples as enticing as David's were all flashing at her! *Settle down my heart! You belong to someone else!*

After class he officially introduced himself and walked her to the library. Evidently, Jesse equated lab partners to classroom buddies -- because he became both. Not a good idea! Getting whiffs of his cologne or accidently brushing against his sculptured body not only disrupted Callie's concentration but stirred up butterflies that she thought were David's alone. And were the seats getting closer ... every class? Maybe it was just the man that was so unsettling. He was definitely unpredictable. The second week of classes he added escorting her to the library to his duties and by the third week he was studying with her at her favorite spot in Bizzell Library.

Callie quickly recognized that her sophomore year wasn't going to be as tranquil as her first one. Biology and Jesse had eliminated that possibility. But he added another dimension. Football. The Sooners were the defending national football co-champs and all eyes in the nation were on the boys in red and white to see if they could take it all this year. Football fever dominated the campus and knowing a first string wide receiver made the games personal, as well as thrilling.

Every Monday after a home game, Jesse quizzed Callie about the game. Then he'd diagram a play for her to watch for in the next game. She and Heather would study it. When they spotted it during a game, they made up their own creative dances of celebration. At least two girls on campus were learning there is method in all that seeming madness on the field. Football was becoming an extracurricular activity ... with Jesse as the instructor.

In the midst of the unsettling challenges, Callie kept a steady stream of letters going between Norman and Charlottesville. David was faithful to call. Callie made no reference to Jesse. Some things in life are difficult to explain.

Callie knew that football demanded much of Jesse, but he carried his share of the biology lab projects. He was not only a promising young athlete, he was an astute biology student. He alleged that came from ranch life. She had to admit Jesse was one gorgeous asset ... academically speaking, of course.

The better acquainted they became, the more he reminded her of Carla. Spontaneous, uninhibited and out-front about almost everything. Fun to be with ... if you didn't mind embarrassing surprises. Being discreet was alien to his personality. Lately another Carla trait was surfacing. That boy could ask more questions than a precocious four year old. And they were getting personal.

"Callie, do you believe there is intelligent design behind all this stuff we are studying or do you attribute it to chance?"

"The former, and I believe that designer's name is God. Why do you ask?"

"Just curious. What do you believe about Jesus' claims to be the Son of God?"

"That answer didn't come as easily as the first for me. Creation shouts of order and design, so believing that there was a God behind it all has never been a struggle. Believing that Jesus was the Christ? That involved a more personal journey into his claims and those who refute them. We don't have enough time to go into it all, but yes, I believe that Jesus was who He claimed to be ... the Son of God. The first chapter of the gospel of John tells us He was in the beginning with God."

Jesse didn't let the subject drop. He picked it up again as he walked her to the library and escorted her to their favorite study spot. Her fun-loving lab partner was not a shallow thinker.

A few day later, he picked another topic. "Callie, tell me about your family." She shared about hers and then asked about his.

"I'm the oldest of six, live on a ranch about seventy-five miles from campus and am on a football scholarship." He told hilarious stories relating to his rather large family and then confessed his love affair with football. "How did you end up at OU, Callie?"

She shared about her academic scholarship and the desire to see and experience more than the mountains and valleys of Virginia.

He reached for her left hand and rubbed his thumb over her ring. "That's quite a ring, Callie. Tell me about it."

She jerked her hand out of his. She didn't like the feelings his touch stirred, but she welcomed the invitation to talk about David and their upcoming marriage. "That's my engagement ring, Jesse. David and I are getting married July 16th."

He took a deep breath and ran his fingers through his short, curly, mess-proof hair. "That's a double whammy! Engaged? Married? You're not coming back next year, are you?"

She shook her head.

"Is your David rich or a Virginia blueblood? That's a very unusual engagement ring."

"David, rich? No. He's a senior on a basketball scholarship at the University of Virginia and works for his dad when not in school. His dad is a local businessman and makes good money. But none of that will be David's until Uncle Joseph dies, and he is a healthy middle-aged man. Besides, David didn't buy this ring. His mother and great-grandmother wore it before me. His mom died when he was a freshman in college."

His gaze was almost immobilizing. She had to redirect his thoughts. "Do you have a girlfriend, Jesse?"

"No, it seems I'm still looking. How long have you and David dated?"

"Since my sixteenth birthday. Over three years now. I've never dated anyone else, Jesse."

"You've never wanted to date anyone else? Ever?"

"Nope. Never."

He reacted as though she had physically slapped his face. "I need to get ready for my next class. See you later." And he gathered his books and walked out of the library … quietly.

Callie was relieved. *Now he knows about David … and our wedding.*

## Chapter 15

Though Jesse's conversation with Callie had put a slight strain in their relationship, they managed to get their projects done. Jesse had pulled back, but enjoyed being with her too much to simply walk away. He was facing a new quandary. He hadn't had a problem attracting a girl of interest … until now. Most of the time he was running from instead of pursuing. Now he had found one he liked … really liked … and she wasn't interested … or available. He had never paid much attention to Murphy's Law.

Common sense urged him to accept the facts she had presented. His heart protested and he was caught in the middle.

The large enrollment at OU made his chances of seeing her next semester unlikely and improbable. By the time the semester was nearing an end, Jesse had made up his mind to risk one more serious conversation with his magnetic lab partner. It was now or never. He opted for now.

As he was walking her to the library after class the next day, he took the leap. "Cal, would you mind if we talk out here before you go in?" She half-heartedly agreed and he led her to a nearby bench. He began by telling her about a list their youth pastor had helped them compose when they were seniors in high school. "Each person worked up a list of fifteen requirements or desired traits they were looking for in a future mate." He pulled a folded, rather wrinkled piece of paper out of his pocket and waved it around.

She laughed and asked to see it. He refused and put it back in his pocket. "After we finished our list, Daniel, our youth pastor, challenged us to quit casual dating. He emphasized that every date has the potential of becoming our future mate. That was a scary thought. I had dated some girls I would never consider marrying. Since completing my list, I've not dated any girl longer than six weeks. When it becomes obvious that they aren't going to get close to my benchmark, I back off."

"Hmm. Your list intrigues me. So you actually rank the girls?"

He laughed. "Yeah, but don't tell. I've dated a couple of sevens, but I've been looking for a number eight girl for almost two years now." His eyes were filled with mischief. "Callie, I know you attend our football games, but are you athletic? Do you enjoy other sports? How about horses? Do you enjoy riding?"

She chuckled. "You give new meaning to discreet, Jesse, but I'll play your game. Dad didn't have any boys, but he made sure his girls knew how to play or enjoy most sports. I grew up a tomboy." She paused and looked at her ring. "David has some beautiful horses and riding is one of our favorite ways to spend time together." She smiled at him and held up her ring. "I love the man who gave me this ring, Jesse, and I'm more than ready to marry him."

"While I've accepted that as *your* facts, Callie, they don't change *mine*. From the day I met you, I began comparing you to my list. A few weeks ago, I realized I had found my number eight girl. You are now my reigning list queen and we've never dated. But it's more than that. I care for you as more than a friend. In fact, I've never experienced these kinds of feelings for any girl and I don't know what to do about that."

Shock radiated from her eyes. "Jesse, if I have given you any reason to believe there was a chance for us, I apologize. I knew we had become friends, but I never meant for it to become more. I'm sorry."

"Callie, you're only guilty of being you. My heart simply refuses to accept the fact that God brought you into my life only to take you away. I can't do anything to stop your marriage to David, but if that ring ever comes off your finger, I want you to remember what I've told you today. I'm seriously interested."

"Jesse, not only is this ring *not* coming off, but a matching wedding band is going to join it soon. You have to accept that." She picked up her books and began to move away from the bench.

"I knew this was a risky conversation, but I made the choice to be honest about my feelings and interest in you … and us."

With eyes now flashing with determination, she turned to face him, but kept the distance between them. "Jesse, there-is-no-us! You are a terrific guy and I like you as a friend, but nothing more. God has your list queen out there somewhere. Mark me off your list and start looking again."

"My ears hear your words, but my heart ignores them. I'm sorry, Cal." With an uncharacteristic despondency, Jesse Collins gathered his belongings and walked away.

That encounter inspired her to call Beth about the progress of the wedding plans. Much of the responsibility and burden had fallen on her mom who was faithfully seeing that the checklist items were being addressed in a timely manner. Talking about the wedding helped.

Later she wrote David a long letter. She hadn't heard from him the last couple of weeks. Her dad and Joseph had been attending the home games and reported the Cavaliers were winning often and it looked like playoffs were in their future.

Jesse's blunt admission put a strain between them. With all the lab projects completed, he ceased contact. She felt the loss of his friendship. The semester ended without even a goodbye.

# Chapter 16

As David was driving to the airport to pick up Callie, he reflected on his semester. The basketball team was playing well. Excitement was high among the players and the student body. He was maintaining a good GPA and his personal life had improved. His phone calls and Callie's engaging letters had helped keep his mind focused on their future.

Josie was still a problem, but he had maintained the same attitude and boundaries of the previous semester. It had helped, but being Jake's roommate and teammate made it impossible to completely eliminate her from his life. And like most females, maturing only improved her appeal. It was impossible to be around her and not be aware of her.

He suspected Jake had been divulging information about his habits and patterns. She had cornered him several times and kept inviting him to join her for an overnight rendezvous. Of course he refused, but being out of sight didn't automatically equal being out of mind. He was grateful that God didn't have a limit on the number of times folks could confess. Lately he had used up more than his share. One more semester and no more Josie … just his sweet Callie.

Callie's plane had touched down and she was leading the pack of exiting passengers. David stared. She was sporting a fashionable, new shoulder length hair style. Her shining chestnut brown, full-bodied hair was bouncy … and becoming. "Why didn't you tell me you had a new look?" he asked as she walked into his embrace.

She tiptoed to kiss him. "Do you like it?"

"I liked your longer style, but that was before I saw this one. It's you. Wow! Yes, I like it, but I love my girl more." He traced her jaw line, kissed her soundly and grabbed her hand before he embarrassed them both. "Let's get your luggage and head home. We have much to talk about."

They chatted all the way to her house and till the last minute of curfew that night. The outside world was not center stage in their lives this break. Wedding plans and conversations about a life together occupied most of their discussions and family ones as well. They were rarely apart except to sleep at night. An early snowfall found them on the slopes a couple of times. Being alone was becoming more challenging. They wisely limited those temptations.

The Cavaliers had two scheduled games over the holidays. One away and one at home. David left a week before Callie's return flight. She had tried to book a later flight back so she could attend his home game, but none was available. David breathed an inward sigh of relief. Josie and Callie at the same game produced fear in his heart.

They parted eager for their next meeting in May.

# Chapter 17

Josie wasn't being as assertive this semester. True, she was at all the home games, like his dad, but other than cheer for him and Jake, she had backed off. Was it possible she had finally gotten his message or had found another interest? One can always hope.

The Cavaliers made it through March and were given a berth in the ACC playoffs. They had a five day window. Coach told them to take a two day break and come back rested and prepared to work hard. David could have gone home, but Callie wasn't there, so he didn't.

Jake mentioned that he was going home for some home cooking, relaxation and a restful night's sleep. He invited David to join him. That was enticement to a tired and hungry athlete who had worked rigorously this semester. Since Josie had backed off, he decided to drop in for a visit. He opted to drive his own vehicle, in case he needed to make a quick exit.

He wasn't surprised that Josie showed up, but he was disappointed. That meant he could not spend the night. He would stay through dinner, spend the evening playing some pool with Jake or his dad and head back to school.

After the deliciously satisfying meal, Jake's folks announced they needed to take the leftovers to a sick friend. That left the college students. Jake and David were in the game room when Jake announced that he had to run to the pharmacy to pick up a prescription for his dad. "It won't take long. We'll play some pool when I get back, Roomie." When the reality hit him that he was in the house alone with Josie, he reasoned that someone would be back soon. He grabbed a pool cue and began to rack the balls.

Five minutes later Josie sauntered into the game room and suggested watching some television and sharing popcorn until the folks got back. He volunteered to pop the corn. He found their popper with a stirring handle. *Maybe I won't scorch it this time.*

The popcorn turned out perfect. With a pleased smile he filled a bowl and headed downstairs to the game room. The TV was on and he could see Josie's head peaking out above the sofa. She had looked especially tempting this evening. He would have to be careful.

As he made his turn to hand her the bowl, he stopped dead in his tracks. Josie had changed clothes … if you could call what she was wearing clothing. He had often wondered what a woman's body looked like unclothed. Now he knew … and it was breath taking. And she was so close. His internal alarms were blaring. He knew he should run … but he couldn't take his eyes off what was being offered. And as if they had been summoned, all those word pictures she had painted over the past two years came rushing across his mind like a stampeding herd of cattle stirring up the dust of former lust.

*Run,* an inner voice shouted. Josie stood up and took the bowl of popcorn from his hand. *Run now,* the voice pleaded. But his body screamed louder as she pressed close and lust consumed his will to resist. He surrendered and the natural desires of a man plus two years of resisting gave way to unbridled passion.

David's gift of virginity to his future wife was forfeited that night though that was not on his mind at the time. The euphoric gratification of his flesh suppressed all else. His youthful lust was pleased and relieved and satisfied … for the time being. Now he knew what he had missed. He was not yet aware of what he had lost.

Sometime later they heard a vehicle pull in the driveway. David grabbed his clothes and hurried to Jake's room to shower. Josie disappeared to hers.

As soap and water began to clean the outer man, the washcloth brushed past his ID bracelet and the pleasure of the evening began to drown in guilt as Callie's face flashed on the screen of his conscience.

God's admonitions and warnings regarding sex outside of marriage began to run like a ticker tape beneath her image. *Shun youthful lust and flee from them. Shun immorality and all sexual looseness – flee from impurity in thought, word and deed.* His dad's voiced warning supplied the audio. *When lust is winning, it indicates a lacking in your relationship with God.*

*Callie! Oh God, I have sinned and betrayed my Callie!* Guilt, regret, shame and fear were vying for attention. *Why did I come? Why did I stay when left alone with her? God, why didn't I run? My spirit was willing … but not my flesh.*

Jake came into the bedroom as David was drying off and getting into his clothes. "Worked up a sweat playing pool, David?" Jake laughed. "Josie won, didn't she? When she found out the folks were going to be gone a couple of hours, she asked me to vanish as well. Figured that's what she had in mind. Now you know, good Buddy, what you have been missing all these years." Jake slapped David on the back and turned on the radio which was playing a new, sensual love song.

David turned several shades of red and Jake smiled. "Don't be embarrassed, Henderson. I'll bet Josie is ecstatic. She may be my sister, but that girl is a ten. You know that better than I do, don't you?"

David didn't respond. He was disgusted with himself. He had been set up and had played the fool. He finished dressing and left Jake in his room.

As politely as possible under the circumstances, he thanked Jake's folks for their hospitality the past three years. Without an explanation to Josie or Jake, he returned to school immediately. He had one day to get honest with himself and God before Jake and Josie returned to campus.

# Chapter 18

True repentance is rare, but like the Psalmist whose name he carried, David wept his way back to God. Psalm 51 became his. *Create in me a clean heart, O God, and renew a steadfast spirit within me.* God's forgiveness was immediate and complete. Forgiving himself and seeking Callie's forgiveness were going to be more challenging. Could she forgive him? Probably not immediately. Would she forgive him? Completely? He was struggling to forgive himself. Why should he expect her to react any differently? Maybe she didn't have to know.

He had to find out what his dad meant about lust not being his root problem, because right now he was reaping a bumper crop. If he didn't discover the root, it was going to consume him and destroy his relationship with Callie … and who knew where it would end?

During his time of confession and repentance, Solomon's warning of the *little foxes that spoil the vineyards of love that are in full bloom* exploded with understanding. His and Callie's love was nearing full bloom with marriage just around the corner. He had tolerated the little foxes of lust, pride and resentment to invade his heart at times the last two years. They had grown up and done significant damage. With God's help he was removing those foxes and seeking the Lord for restoration of the losses.

He called a realtor his dad knew and made arrangements to rent an efficiency off campus for the rest of the semester. He was in the midst of packing when Jake walked in. "Hey, Roomie. What are you doing?" Without waiting for an answer he continued. "And why did you leave so quickly? Josie was looking forward to spending the weekend with you. I've never seen her so happy."

"Look, Jake. What happened Friday was a big mistake. I'm really sorry and I promise you it won't happen again. I'm moving out of yours and Josie's lives. She's too much to resist on my own."

"Moving out of our lives? Too much to resist? Won't happen again? Are you crazy? Josie Roberts is one of the hottest babes on this campus and you know it. Don't ask me why, but you turn her on. And if you'd get honest, you'd have to admit you've wanted her for the last two years. Why fight it, David? She's yours for the taking. She's not only beautiful; she's smart and fun. You two are perfect for each other."

"Sorry, Jake. It's not Josie I want; it's Callie. I'm moving out today."

Jake exploded and contaminated the air with his thoughts. He stormed out of the room, picked up the hall phone and called Josie. Talking loud enough for anyone still on their wing to hear, he gave his version of what was happening. "Forget the weasel who used you, Sis. He's a loser." There was a pause. "Sure he was passionate. You were his first, remember? Now his guilty conscience has him packing up and moving out." Another pause. "You're right. There's nothing to feel guilty about, but he does." Silence. "There's nothing wrong with you, Josie. He's the problem. Call someone who appreciates you. Don't mope over this holy Joe."

When Jake came back into the room, David addressed the other problem between them. "Jake, these playoffs are bigger than us and our differences. We can't carry them onto the court."

"Don't you think it's a little late to be thinking about that? I don't know if I can handle your piety on or off the court."

"I'm not blaming any of this on you or Josie. This has all been my fault."

That statement caught Jake off guard and he walked out of the room. David finished packing and headed to his new residence. This was a move he should have made three years ago.

Practice started the next day and Jake had mellowed some. "David, we've played together four years and we're both better players because of the other. I may not like you as a person right now, but I do respect what you bring to this team. I'm willing to put our differences aside for the rest of the season for the sake of the team and our school."

"Me too, Jake." They shook hands and allowed the love of the game and the goals before them to dictate their behavior. Other than practice and games, they wouldn't be seeing each other anyway. David was grateful.

Living alone gave David time and freedom to think, seek the Lord and listen. Being intimate with Josie had unleashed a horde of lust. Forgiveness was one thing, but he needed to be free from the power of the desire that was now consuming him so he didn't have to keep repenting of the same sins over and over again.

The need to quit lying to himself and God became evident. He had to become transparent ... spiritually naked so to speak. So he faced the ugly truth. Lust uses another person to satisfy one's own personal needs and desires. Love protects and honors the other person above his own needs and desires. A verse from I Corinthians 13 began to roll through his mind. *Love does not dishonor others, it is not self-seeking.*

He concluded that unless God's unselfish love is involved in a relationship, then selfishness will dominate. Dad was right. The pieces were coming together. His lust problem stemmed from a lack of relationship with God ... the source of unselfish love.

*Lord, what does a relationship with You look like?*

## Chapter 19

When Joseph heard the Cavaliers made the playoffs, he called Callie. "David is part of UV basketball history. I'm going to the first game. Want to meet me there?"

"Oh, yes!"

"Good, I've arranged air flights for both of us to meet at the Washington National Airport near Landover. Let's surprise him." She agreed and plans were made.

David called Callie the next day to tell her about making the playoffs. She was a good keeper of secrets ... and so was he.

Arrangements to miss classes the day of the flight had been made and Heather dropped Callie off at the Will Rogers Airport. She arrived at Washington National an hour before Joseph. He rented a car and they headed to the Capital Centre Arena. He had booked red eye flights back for both of them.

Their arena seats were ten rows behind the team bench. It had been almost three months since Callie had seen David. Her stomach was in knots and she kept fidgeting with her ring while waiting for his team to emerge from the locker room. When she saw him, she had to restrain herself from jumping up and calling his name. Instead, she leaned forward as the butterflies flitted back and forth between her heart and stomach as she watched him run through the warm-up routines. He was hitting nothing but net from every spot on the court.

She felt remorse for missing all his games the last two seasons. Seeing him in this setting reminded her of the hardship her choice of schools had put on their relationship. But there are no do-overs in life and their days of separation were almost over.

Five rows in front of them sat a family that kept cheering for Jake and David by name. A strikingly beautiful sister or girlfriend was the most animated. Callie remembered seeing her a few times when she had attended his weekend home games.

David was so focused on the drills that Callie was beginning to wonder if he would ever spot them. When the drills ended, he walked to the bench to pick up a towel, lifted his eyes to glance at Jake's family and spotted his dad. The smile that had been sunshine to her heart for years lit up his face. He spoke to one of his coaches and headed up the aisle. *Pretty Girl* called his name as he walked passed her row, but he kept moving. She turned to track his destination. Callie lifted her eyes and noticed David's *deer blinded by on coming headlights* stare. She was pleased. She had surprised him.

After regaining his composure, he casually hugged them and made plans to meet after the game. Still a little stunned and seemingly at a loss for words, David excused himself and returned to a night of history in the making.

The cheerleader in row five waited until David was back on the court, then climbed over the folks between her and the aisle and headed their way. She smugly introduced herself as David's girlfriend and asked who they were.

Callie was dumbfounded and looked at Joseph for help. Without missing a beat, he politely introduced himself as David's dad and Callie as David's fiancée. The alleged girlfriend checked out Callie's ring finger and with uncommon audacity asserted, "I'm Josie. It's good to finally meet you, Callie." With an air of satisfaction and accomplishment, she sashayed back to her seat.

Callie wasn't sure her heart was still beating. Shock prevented any response. The butterflies were devoured by consuming disbelief. She sat there! Watching David. Looking at Girlfriend's back. *David's girlfriend? He told Josie about me, yet I've heard nothing about her.*

As his team headed back to the locker room, he glanced at Callie and their eyes locked. David Henderson's eyes betrayed him. She broke the connection and both of them looked at Josie who threw him a kiss and waved. He looked away and dejectedly followed his team off the court.

Fourteen weeks before their wedding and something was very wrong. She couldn't watch him play tonight with his self-proclaimed girlfriend in her peripheral vision. She looked at his ring and fingered the heart pendant close to her own. The tears she had tried to keep at bay crashed through her barrier.

On her finger was their future. She clutched it tightly for a few minutes as the tears increased, then removed and placed it carefully in Joseph's hand. She unclasped the necklace and added it to the collection. "I can't stay. I'll call a taxi and head back to the airport. We can meet when the game is over. I think our planes leave about the same time. I'm so sorry." She hugged him and headed up the aisle for the exit.

Joseph didn't comment or try to stop her. He was dealing with his own anger and disappointment. *Guess the lust won, Lord. Help my son ... and that bride and daughter that just walked out of our lives.*

Callie managed to get a cab to the airport and found a quiet spot to retreat. The tears were relentless. The shock was wearing off but heartrending pain was moving in. *Evidently, he found someone else and didn't have the courage to tell me. He's been more honest with her than he has with me.* Grief and anguish previously unknown to Callie Adams began to consume her. Her heart was shattered. Her future unknown.

# CHAPTER 20

When the team returned for the game, David looked at his father and saw the empty seat. No Callie! Panic had set in when he first saw her. He thought he would die on the spot when he saw Josie talking to them. But he knew the most incriminating evidence for Callie had been his own guilty response. His heart began to beat erratically, his mind shifted into overdrive and an army of emotions began dueling for supremacy.

"Where is she?" He mouthed to his dad as he pointed to the empty seat.

"Gone." His dad mouthed back and then held up the engagement ring.

David's world crashed at his feet. *NO!* There was no way he could play ball when his life and future were falling apart. He wanted to strangle Josie who was still keeping an eagle eye on him.

Without a second thought, he went to his coach and told him a family crisis had occurred and he needed to leave with his dad. They talked a few minutes and the coach released him from the game. David leaped up the steps and asked his dad to meet him at the south entrance in fifteen minutes. Anxiously he ran to the locker room, showered, dressed and hurried to meet Joseph.

"What is going on, Dad? Where is Callie? Why do you have her ring?" He was desperate for answers.

Joseph responded with his characteristic calmness though his eyes were betraying his concern. "I think you are the one with some questions to answer, Son. Why did the attractive young lady I've seen at every home game cheering for you and Jake decide to introduce herself as your girlfriend to me and your fiancée? Why would Josie tell Callie she was glad to finally meet her? How is it that the two of you know each other so well? Maybe those are the questions that need answering first."

David knew he had been caught and he felt both regret and relief. He had come clean with God. Maybe it was time to come clean with the folks that mattered most in his life. Immediately a verse from James surfaced. *Confess your faults to one another and pray for one another ... that you may be healed.*

*I have confessed to You, Lord. I'll humble myself and confess to Dad and Callie and become accountable to them as well. I'm in desperate need of healing.*

His dad's composure fortified his will to confess. "How did you get here and where is Callie, Dad?"

"Callie and I flew into Washington National. I have a rental. She took a taxi back to the airport where she has a red eye connection back to Oklahoma City tonight. My plane leaves about the same time as hers. We've got roughly a four hour window."

"Then let's head to the airport. I need to talk with both of you. You and I can talk on the way. I'll try to find a place to talk with her there."

As his dad drove, David shared the saga of the last three years with Josie. He didn't go into details but he was honest and contrite. Joseph listened. "What am I going to tell Callie, Dad?"

"Why don't you stick with the truth, Son? It's obvious that you are repentant and have made some needed changes to avoid a repeat. That's a good place to start. I don't hear excuses or blame. I see you taking responsibility for your choices and behavior. I believe Callie will see your heart."

His dad placed the ring in David's hand. "I have her necklace in my other pocket. I don't know what her response will be, but I doubt she will be wearing either of these when she boards her plane tonight. So prepare yourself."

David and Joseph prayed together before entering the airport. "Dad, I'm beginning to believe your statement about lust and my lack of relationship with God."

David spotted Callie and took the empty seat beside her. Joseph excused himself. Neither spoke for a few minutes. Witnessing Callie's pain gave personal insight into God's guidelines regarding sex outside of marriage.

"What are you doing here, David? Your team needs you."

Her eyes were already red and swollen from crying but it was the look of utter disbelief that pierced his heart. "I couldn't play, Callie. When Dad showed me your ring …" He was struggling for control. "Nothing, including a playoff game, is worth losing you."

"But we could have talked another time."

"No! I would have been a liability. This is not an ideal place, but we need to talk now."

Callie pointed to the far corner of an almost empty waiting area. He grabbed her hand as they changed locations. Callie's fear of his untold story was palpable, yet she was giving him a chance to explain. "Who is she, David?"

"Callie, Dad told me what Josie said to you." He reached for both hands. "First, she is not my girlfriend, never has been and never will be. You are my forever girl and I have loved only you. I beg you to believe that." Then with regret that matched her pain, he confessed. "Josie is Jake's younger sister."

He knew that announcement would rock her world. "You have known her for four years?" With a look of utter dismay she confronted him. "I cannot believe this. Four years! I never once doubted your faithfulness or honesty, David. Not once! As much as I don't want to hear it, you owe me the truth."

He nodded and then told a condensed version of Josie's involvement in his life. He didn't excuse any of his choices or behavior. He didn't point a finger of blame at Callie. He was honest. He was repentant. He was broken.

Witnessing the price Callie was paying for his relationship with Josie was bad enough, but there was more. "Callie, until recently, the battles had all been in my mind and the involvement emotional." She stopped him.

"Have you ... have the two of you ... been ... physically intimate, David?"

*God in heaven, how could I have done this to her?* "Once ... two weeks ago. I have had no contact with her since then ... until the game tonight.

His Callie turned her back to him and her body began to tremble. She moved out of her chair and walked away. Any remnant of pleasure that night had afforded him became bitter dregs. Turning to face him, she asked between sobs, "Obviously you have feelings for her, David. Or has this all been about ... lust?"

"The latter, Callie." He told of Josie's many offers and the night of her setup and seduction ... and his sin. "I moved out of the dorm and out of their lives that night. I know that was three years too late."

Her tear flow never slowed but her countenance softened some. "She was why you wanted to get married two years ago, wasn't she?"

"Yes."

He watched as hurt and anger battled in her. "Why didn't you tell me, David? I've known girls like her since high school. I wouldn't have been upset with you. I would've understood and hopefully made some different choices. Why did you try to deal with her by yourself?" She shook her head as though she couldn't take anymore and sat down.

David dropped to his knees in front of her and with tears pooling in his deep-set, brown repentant eyes, he humbled himself. "I'm asking you to forgive me, Callie. I have betrayed your trust and violated our love and commitment. I know God has forgiven me. Can you?"

She turned her head and stared out the large windows where the planes were lining up on the runway. She was quiet a long time.

When she faced him again, a cloud of grief and loss was clinging to her like a heavy August fog. "When did you to plan to tell me all this, David? Or were you going to marry me without saying a word?" She waited for his answer.

"To be honest, I hadn't decided."

With more boldness than he knew she possessed, she responded. "There are two issues here, and you have only faced one of them until tonight. After three years of struggling and a night of passion, you finally got honest with yourself and God about Josie. But it took a God setup to make you face your dishonesty and deception with me. Both were wrong, David."

He had asked God if he should tell her. He had his answer. Honesty and trust are key to relationships. She was right. Both lust and deception were wrong. "From this moment on, I promise you there'll be no more secrets between us. I will be honest and accountable with you and Dad for the rest of my life. Please forgive me for dishonesty as well as lust, Callie."

"It's going to take some time, David. Put yourself in my place for a minute. How would you react or respond if the shoe was on the other foot tonight?"

The images that question invoked were his undoing. Even the thought of her being as unfaithful and deceptive to him as he had been to her for three years unnerved him so much he felt nauseated. What would the reality of it do?

"It would totally shatter me, Callie. Sweet Jesus, it would be worse than losing my mom. What have I done to you? To us?"

He moved close and pulled her into his arms. She slumped against him and tried to smother the deep sobs. He held her tight and kept repeating. "I am so sorry, Callie. I am so sorry."

He moved her back to a seat and knelt before her again. "Callie, please look at me." The eyes that met his were now veiled. "I want you to know Mom's ring will never belong to anyone else. Is there any chance I can put it back on your finger tonight and we can work through the mess I've made of our relationship? I won't rush you for a wedding date. You can take all the time you need."

"Not tonight ... and maybe not ever!" Callie put her head in her hands and the torrents came.

David's own tears were no longer contained. She was closing him out.

"May I call you when we get back to our schools?"

"No. Please don't."

Two strikes. He wasn't willing to risk a third one. He kissed her on the forehead. "I have to get back to the hotel. We have curfew during the tournament. I'll be waiting to hear from you. Please don't shut me out permanently, Callie." He hugged her again and walked away experiencing a darkness of his soul that rivaled the night surrounding him.

Like Jake's shower, his taxi ride became another place of confession and repentance. A verse from Galatians came to light. *Do not be deceived: God cannot be mocked. A man reaps what he sows.* His harvest was one of loss and ruin. *Father, I've also read where you take the ashes of our lives and turn them into places and things of beauty. I give you my harvest of ashes tonight. Only You can turn this around.*

The Cavaliers won their game that night. David joined them for the next games and UV won the ACC championship that season for the first time in the history of the program. They advanced to the national playoffs and were defeated by DePaul in the first round. That loss was miniscule compared to the personal loss David was facing.

# CHAPTER 21

By the time her plane touched down at Will Rogers Airport, Callie had replayed the entire night multiple times. The thought of David being intimate with another woman shredded her in ways she couldn't describe. His dishonesty and deception the last three years were just as disturbing. The knowledge that Josie's quest had been unrelenting stirred a small amount of understanding.

Suddenly it hit her that a broken engagement means the wedding has to be cancelled. *How am I going to explain any of this to my parents and friends?*

She was still wrestling with possible answers to that issue when Heather met her in the early morning hours. "Merciful heavens, Callie. What happened to you?"

"I guess you could say I got slam dunked, Heather. I'm not ready to talk about it, yet." So Heather drove and Callie cried.

She called her mom later that day and told her the wedding had been called off. Beth was speechless. "Yes, Mom. All plans need to be cancelled. Just tell folks it's on hold for a while." Her mom pressed for answers, but Callie offered nothing more. "Not now, Mom. We'll talk when I get home."

The missing ring triggered numerous episodes of weeping the first few days. In time she shared with Heather about the broken engagement and cancelled wedding. She didn't offer any reasons.

Callie was well aware that she was an emotional wreck, physically exhausted from lack of sleep and struggling mentally to focus and concentrate. She had no clue how to cope with the life changing events that she was now facing.

# Chapter 22

David's collegiate basketball career ended with the 69 - 60 loss to DePaul on March 25th and he hadn't seen Jake since the 26th. There had been no contact with Josie since Callie's surprise appearance. Graduation was scheduled for May 15th. David knew there was unfinished business between him and the Roberts siblings so he set up a meeting in a private study room of the library.

Jake was civil, but solemn. Josie was flirty and cocky. The atmosphere was charged. "Thank you for coming." *Lord, help me be honest but kind.* "I wanted a chance to apologize to both of you. We've been together four years and have shared some good times, and though we have much in common, we have one crucial difference. Our belief system. Both of you have been open and honest about yours. I have not. My reasons were lame and wrong.

"Simply put, I believe that *in the beginning God.* Since I believe He is our Creator and Designer, I also choose to believe that His guidelines for the way we live our lives are far wiser than any I could come up with. That was the basis for my choice of abstinence until marriage.

"Josie, you are a beautiful and desirable woman. That was no excuse for dishonoring you. And by dishonoring you, I have betrayed Callie. I love her and intend to keep myself sexually pure from this time forward ... whether she ever agrees to marry me or not."

Josie spoke up with a challenging tone in her voice. "What if told you that I was pregnant with your baby? How would that news affect your God and your belief system we are hearing about?"

David went pale. But here again was a consequence of his choice. "Are you pregnant with my baby, Josie?"

"Well, I've missed one period and I'm pretty sure it's yours if I am. So what do you plan to do about it?"

This was evidently news to Jake. "Well, you don't have to worry about it, Sis. If you are, Mom and Dad will pay for an abortion. Women don't have to carry unwanted babies anymore."

Josie smiled. "David wouldn't like that, would you, David?"

"No, I wouldn't, even if it's not mine."

"A baby changes everything, doesn't it, David?" Josie asked with confidence.

"Josie, a baby means I am going to be responsible for a child's life. It doesn't mean I am going to change my mind about a future with you. If you don't want the baby, I will take it. If you keep it, I will help with the finances and be as much a part of its life as possible. I'll also be honest with Callie."

Josie was angry. "You want the baby, but not me. Is that what you are saying?"

"Well, as harsh as that sounds, yes, that's what I'm saying."

Josie looked at Jake and stomped out. Jake looked at David and followed Josie.

David didn't move for a long time. Any chance he had with Callie probably just got knocked off the radar.

# Chapter 23

Heather alerted Jesse that David's ring was missing ... in case he was still interested. The impossible had happened. He had not seen Callie since their last discouraging conversation months ago. Still interested? Is the parched prairie interested in the possibility of rain?

"How is she, Heather?"

"I'm worried about her, Jesse. That's why I called. She should be in the library within the hour. I thought you might want to stop by."

He wasted no time. She wasn't in her usual spot. So he cruised the floors and wings until he caught a glimpse of her. The table resembled a cotton field ready for picking with a human head thrown in the midst. *Either she's crying a lot or she's been here a long time.*

Quietly he approached and lightly placed a hand on her shoulder. She jerked and looked up. Tears were abundant. She grabbed another tissue and blew and wiped, enlarging her cotton yield. She put her head back down and her shoulders began to shake.

Growing up in a house of six males and only two females, Jesse wasn't accustomed to weeping women, but this was Callie ... he couldn't walk away. He moved a chair close and placed his arm around her shoulders. She raised her head, grabbed another Kleenex and blew and wiped and covered another empty spot on the table with evidence of her pain. But this time she leaned in and cried harder. He was pleased with the leaning in, but wasn't sure what to do about the increased liquid output.

One look confirmed that the ring that had kept her out of his reach was gone and he was experiencing joy in the midst of her white field of grief. That make him feel guilty … but not for long. He'd help her get over her sadness. He wanted to dance but knew this was not the time.

Suddenly Callie pulled away and apologized for being so weepy. She was making every effort to get control and divert both from the topic that was hanging heavily between them.

Jesse reached over and gently touched her ring finger. "What happened, Cal?"

"I'll be okay, Jesse. I just need time."

"What you need is a friend to talk to. Why can't it be me?"

Reluctantly, she lifted her face until their eyes met. "You can trust me, Callie. I'm not going to hurt you."

She studied his face quietly and then began to relate the events of that fateful evening. He watched her fight for control during the telling. When she got to David's betrayal, she broke. Jesse, though battling two contrasting emotions, sat quietly. He wanted to pulverize the two-timing scalawag for hurting Callie and then thank him for being so stupid.

When she was calm enough to continue, she shared about David's deep sorrow and brokenness and his wish for reconciliation. She didn't have to say anymore. That meant she was the one who broke the engagement. First Joy! Now Hope!

His feet kept begging to dance and his heart was aching to hold his wounded list queen. In fact, he was going to risk the latter. "Callie, let's grab your things and go for a walk. It's a cool, clear evening and we'll find a bench somewhere quiet. We don't have to talk. What do you say?"

She looked at him, and as though she had down shifted into slow motion, began to put her books and papers in her bag. She added a half empty box of tissue to the collection. He filled a waste can with the remnants of her misery. His hand found hers and hung on. She needed a friend and he was volunteering.

As they neared her dorm, Jesse pointed to an empty bench. Callie sat down and he joined her. Without any hesitation, he put his arm around her and pulled her close. She rested her head on his welcoming shoulder. And he clutched her a little tighter.

Quickly the softness of her body against his muscular frame began to awaken the physical attraction he had sequestered for over a year. And before he could corral that distraction, some delicate, exotic floral scent launched an attack on his brain cells. His heart began to mimic one of those Indian pow-wow drums some of his native friends play while waves of affection long restrained began to wash on the shores of his heart, saturating him with desire. He was thunderstruck and out-with-it Jesse had to get it out. "Callie, I need to tell you something."

"Okay."

"I know it's too soon to talk about it, but I want you to know you are still my reigning list queen. I've dated since we last talked, but none for long."

She didn't move but softly questioned. "Still number eight, huh?" He drew her closer and tightened his embrace.

"Yes!" With every breath he was freeing hopes and dreams he had kept corralled in a small corner stall of his heart. Tonight he opened the barn door and let them run free.

A good hour passed. Jesse stirred a little. Exhausted Callie had dozed. She woke and stretched. "Thanks, Jesse. I do need a friend. Thanks for not pushing or trying to move in but also being honest. You're right. I'm not ready for any of that stuff you talked about, but I am hung up on honesty in relationships." She moved out of his private space. "I need to get back to the dorm and finish this paper. Would you walk me the rest of the way?"

They walked in silence. Before Jesse turned to leave, she kissed him lightly on the cheek and walked away.

As he watched her disappear in the maze of people and hallways, he marveled over the outcome of the day. Something he had never experienced before became apparent. Love for a woman. He was in love with his list queen, and he knew his life would never be the same.

His celebration was short lived. Though friendly, Callie did not allow a repeat of that night. In fact, she put a halter on his hopes and dreams and put them back in the corral. She wasn't ready. He didn't like it, but he understood.

Heather kept him informed of her progress. He was close by more times than she knew. He did drop in Bizzell some and occasionally showed up for a meal. She wasn't over David yet, but at least she had quit planting new cotton fields every time she studied. Jesse hoped her heart was mending, because he had lost his.

# Chapter 24

Graduation neared and David was bombarded with a plethora of emotions and thoughts. Earning his degree and moving into the work force was exciting. But as much as he loved home, he dreaded facing the questions regarding his and Callie's break-up. His dad said Beth was telling folks the wedding had been put on hold. Nothing had been mentioned about the broken engagement or his involvement with Josie.

Joseph had been his mainstay and accountability partner since Callie's departure from his life. And as hard as it was to admit, he was glad his mom didn't have to deal with his indiscretions. But then he wondered if her influence and input would have made a difference in his involvement with Josie. He'd never know.

John and Beth joined Joseph for David's graduation. Callie was still in school. He hadn't expected her to attend, but he had hoped she would call or send a card in response to the announcement he sent. She did neither. Her silence was deafening.

On top of that, he had received an unexpected card from Josie informing him she had aborted *his* baby. He was possibly the father of a child ... now in heaven. Hopefully his mom was on nursery duty. David was learning that forgiveness doesn't negate earthly consequences.

His fourth day back at work, Joseph alerted him that Callie was on the line. Suddenly his chest felt like it was caught in a vice.

His voice betrayed his anxiety. "Hi ... Cal."

"Hi, David." Her voice was steadier. "How are you?"

"Better now." He took a deep breath. Never had he spoken truer words.

"My plane arrives at Roanoke Regional at 10:00 p.m. tomorrow. Could you pick me up? We need to talk."

"I'll be there."

"Thank you. Will you call Dad and tell him I've asked you to meet me?"

"As soon as we hang up." He paused. "Callie … I love you."

"I know, David. We'll talk tomorrow night. See you then." And she hung up.

David Henderson took a deep breath. A sense of relief that he hadn't known since the night at the airport settled over him. Maybe all was not lost. He called John immediately. Both were surprised but pleased with her change of plans.

## Chapter 25

The sight of David waiting for her initially roused her hibernating butterflies but they were soon restrained by thoughts of his unfaithfulness and dishonesty. *This reunion could have been so different.* And with that thought, tears pooled.

Without asking, he pulled her into a warm embrace. She didn't resist. Neither spoke at first. David broke the silence. "Thank you for tonight. It's been tough not hearing from you and being home without you."

"That's why I asked you to meet me. Let's grab my luggage and talk on the ride home. Okay?"

As she moved out of his embrace, he reached for her hand. Occasional small talk interrupted the silence until they reached his car. "How are you, Callie?"

"Better than the last time we were together."

"God knows how sorry I am for all I've put you through. I'm sure there is much you need to say to me. I promise I'll listen."

She had thought about this conversation many times. "Being with you makes it all seem like a nightmare. I have much more compassion and understanding for folks who deal with this kind of heartache, David."

"Yeah, and I'm not so quick to judge the splinters in someone else's eye since the beams in my own have been exposed."

"I never suspected yours, David. From my youth up, you had been my hero and then I fell in love with you and you became my knight in shining armor. In my mind you were close to perfect. My fairy tale mentality had a head-on collision with reality. My love for you survived, but a lifetime of trust has been wiped out."

His eyes widened as shock and surprise painted his face. "You still love me?"

"Yes, but love is not enough at this point, David. Without trust there can be no relationship."

He reached for her hand and then turned his attention back to the road ahead. "Callie, if you'll give me a chance, I'll earn your trust again."

"Time will tell."

"I'm not going to date anyone else. I'll wait."

"That's your choice, but in the meantime, we need to decide what we tell my parents and others about our breakup."

Approaching this subject brought her near tears. "I've only told my folks that our wedding is on hold. They don't even know about the broken engagement yet, and I have no intention of divulging anything about Josie. Three people in this town know what happened, and as far as I'm concerned, that's enough."

She noted a tear rolling off his cheek and kept quiet. He didn't respond, but turned into the next public parking lot. He turned to face her. "You don't have to do that, Callie. This is all my fault and you don't have to cover my sin."

"I'm not covering your sin. You have confessed to God, your dad and me. I simply refuse to broadcast it to folks who have no need to know and would use it as fodder for the gossip mills."

David studied her for a minute or more before responding. "I'm humbled, Callie." He was struggling to maintain his composure. "What do you suggest we tell your folks and others?"

"First, tell me what you've had to face since returning."

"Except for work, Cal, I've stayed home. I've been too ashamed to interact with folks … even yours. Dad said a few have asked him and he just told them that we have some kinks to work out."

"What if I tell Mom and Dad that both of us formed strong friendships at school that caused me to question the wisdom of staying engaged at this time.."

David stammered, "Callie, I'm confused. Are you telling me there is someone like Josie in your life at OU?"

"Yes and no. I haven't been totally honest with you either, David. Last fall Jesse and I were assigned as biology lab partners. We have become good friends. College friendships happen. I'm using that connection to lighten your involvement with Josie."

"Is Jesse why we won't be dating?"

"Trust and healing are our issues, David."

Without another word, he started the engine and pulled back on the road. Both were quiet for ten or fifteen minutes. "Callie, there's something else I have to tell you. I made you a promise that there would be no more secrets between us and this one may hurt more than the initial truth about Josie."

"What could be crueler than that, David?"

He hesitated several minutes as though weighing his words and their impact. With humility and obvious remorse, David told Callie about his meeting with Jake and Josie ... and the baby and recent news of the abortion.

Callie didn't respond at first. She was allowing the thought of *David's* baby to sink in. His ... but not hers. That did hurt more. "And you only had sex with her one time?"

"God is my witness, Callie. Only the night I told you about." There was desperation in his voice. "Do you believe me?"

"Yes, David, I do."

"Callie, I've learned the importance of truthfulness in relationships, but I'm aware this may be too much truth. Is it? Is there still hope for us?"

They were nearly home. She took a deep breath. "A baby. Aborted. Yours and Josie's. Yeah, that's tough truth to hear." She held back the tears that were determined to come. "But somehow I think it was harder for you to share than for me to hear ... but you did."

She looked out the window for a few minutes. "You chose honesty over our relationship and that lays the foundation for rebuilding trust. Hope? Yes, David, you've just given me hope."

David didn't respond. Callie was fairly certain he was battling his own tears. They were in her driveway now. He cleared his throat. "Callie, I have loved you for years. I know I've given you reason to question that love, but I've never loved you more than I do right now."

His heart was like a powerful magnet drawing her back to him. "Let's be friends and cousins for this summer, David. We'll have many occasions to be together and interact. I'm not shutting you out of my life. I'm just not willing to date you yet."

"It's more than I deserve." He waited for her eyes to meet his. "I've been waiting to hear about your plans for the fall. You're planning to return to OU, aren't you?"

She nodded.

The outside lights were reflecting off his face. If pain and regret could be painted on a human, Callie knew what that would look like.

"Is it possible that you are considering dating Jesse?"

She didn't have plans to tell him any of this. "Yes, David. That's a possibility. He indicated an interest in me when I was engaged, and although I was attracted to him, my heart was yours and I kept my distance. I'm no longer wearing your ring and I'm curious what it would be like to date someone else."

"I know I have no right to question you, but Callie, if you still love me, why would you do that? If there is hope for us, why would you risk that? I'm begging you to reconsider."

"Love wasn't enough the first go around, David. How do I know it will be any different now? I think the pain of your affair has aroused a curiosity in me. I wonder if I could ever have feelings for someone else. Were you ever emotionally involved with Josie?"

*God, I promised to be honest.* "God has forgiven me, but yes, the semester you refused to marry me. Love was never in the mix, but I allowed it to go beyond friendship because of my disappointment and loneliness. Those are excuses, Callie, not good reasons."

"That's why you're concerned about Jesse and me, isn't it?"

"Yes, it puts fear in my heart."

"Jesse is not like Josie. He is a believer with the same boundaries I have."

"Then I have more reason to be concerned. His chances of winning your heart are immense after what I've done."

"Right now, I'm your friend and I'm Jesse's friend. I love you. I am not in love with him." With that, she exited his car and waited for him to set out her luggage. They carried them into the house where her folks were waiting in the living room. She thanked him for picking her up and he politely excused himself.

# Chapter 26

Callie knew why her parents were still awake. Even Carla had joined them. She was a David fan. Callie hugged them and then yielded to the task in front of her.

John took the lead. "What has happened between you and David, Callie? I see you aren't even wearing his ring. One day Joseph told us that the two of you were going to surprise David at the first playoff game. The next day he went silent and you announced the wedding was off. That must have been some surprise."

"It was a revealing trip, Dad." She took a deep breath. "Four years ago David met the sister of his roommate and teammate. The family lives close to campus which allowed David to form a close relationship with all of the family."

"So his surprise was bigger than yours. You met her, didn't you? Was their relationship more than a friendship, Callie?" John's tone indicated he knew the answer to that question.

"Yes, I did meet her. And yes, it was more … on her part."

Beth was troubled. "Are they still in a relationship?"

"No, David had already severed all ties with the girl and her family. She made a desperate attempt to change his mind that night. He wants the marriage to proceed. I'm the one uncomfortable with that right now."

Beth wasn't satisfied with that answer. "Are you the one who broke the engagement, Callie?"

"Yes, Mom, I am. But in all fairness to David, I have to confess that I have developed a friendship with a male student assigned as my biology lab partner last fall."

John jumped back in the conversation. "Did your friend have anything to do with the breaking of your engagement?"

"No."

"Would this young man happen to be a football player who wears the number eighty-five jersey?"

Her forehead wrinkled slightly as her eyes broadcast her surprise. "Yes, Dad. How did you know?"

"Your unusual excitement and informed conversations about the Sooners and game plays which always involved that number, Callie."

"Will you and David still date?" Carla chimed in.

"Not right now."

"Oh, let me guess," Carla interjected. "You've decided to return to OU next year, haven't you?"

"Yes, Carla, I have."

"You'll be free to date others, like your new friend, Jesse, won't you?"

"We will both be free to date others, Carla."

"Bet you David doesn't like this idea," she answered curtly.

"Carla, this is a personal decision and a private problem David and I have to work through. That's why I asked him to pick me up tonight. We haven't talked since the breakup. We had a very productive and encouraging conversation tonight."

"I find this all very interesting," Carla observed. "David will be here, and you and friend Jesse will be there ... free to date. What is wrong with you, Callie?"

John asked Carla to refrain from anymore comments. Callie asked to be excused for the evening and disappeared to her room.

She knew her parents suspected there was more to the story, but out of respect for her they didn't push any further. Carla would push ... and pry. *I never have to wonder where Carla stands on any issue. I can't decide if that is a blessing, a curse -- or just Carla.*

# Chapter 27

It was certainly a different summer for David and Callie, but enough events brought them together that a gentle reconnecting was happening. As the date of their cancelled wedding approached, both were besieged with memories and regrets. David risked a call. "Callie, would you consider one date this summer? Tomorrow would have been our wedding day and I don't think I can face it alone. May we please spend it together?"

"Yes, I'd like that."

They rode horses and fished on the banks of the James, swam in the old swimming hole and went to their favorite restaurant for dinner. Then they drove the parkway to visit a couple of scenic spots along the Blue Ridge. As evening shadows gathered, David pulled into their favorite overlook. Both exited the vehicle and were drawn by the evidence of God's creativity that stretched before them.

David moved behind Callie and pulled her close. She melted in his embrace and placed her arms over his. "I love these mountains, Callie. Their beauty. Their majesty. Their vastness. Their peacefulness."

She leaned her head against his chest. "It's almost like being on holy ground, David. It's one of the few places not contaminated by man."

As the sun sank in the western sky, a scene that only God could paint began to unfold. "Can you believe that sunset?"

She sighed. "I choose to believe He's telling us He cares about our pain."

"Mixed in with my pain and regret is a huge measure of hope and gratitude. God didn't give up on me and I will not give up on us".

Callie turned in his arms and cupped his face in her hands. "I do love you, David Henderson." David tenderly kissed Callie for the first time in months.

A full moon began to rise in the east.

"I promise you I won't blow it the next time you say yes, Callie Adams."

"I'm close to believing that."

Their relationship was strengthened that day and the rest of the summer was a rebuilding of trust.

As the summer neared an end, Callie arranged to meet David at Riverview Park. An afternoon of some serious canoeing but less serious conversation made for a fun time.

As they were walking back to the car, David reached for her hand and pulled her into his arms. Ever so gently, he traced her jawline to her chin and lifted her face until their eyes linked their hearts. For that brief moment, it was as though nothing had ever come between them. His kiss was deep and arousing.

Resting his forehead on hers, he asked, "May I call this semester?"

"Yes, I'd like that."

# Chapter 28

Callie was grateful that her third year roomie was still willing to be her airport chauffeur. From the minute they hugged, the chatter began. Secrets were few. Heather was relieved that Callie's left hand was still ringless. She made it known that she was a Jesse fan.

The girls unpacked, settled in and two days later Callie headed to her first class of the semester. As she walked into the crowded criminal justice classroom, she glanced around looking for a seat. Déjà vu! Nine rows up sat her biology lab partner and he was having the same impact today as he did last fall. He stood up and pointed to the empty seat beside him. Her feet obeyed.

Still speechless, she wiggled past three other students to the empty seat indicated. "Hi, Beautiful! I saved it for you."

She blushed and took her seat as the professor called the class to order. *How did he know I'd be in this class? And what is he doing here?*

After explaining the goals of the Criminal Investigation class, Dr. Hoffman announced that cases would be assigned to pairs. "You may choose your partners or I will assign them." Hands were raised as several students elected to work together. Without looking she knew that Jesse was going to volunteer them. He did.

All the time the professor was discussing requirements and making assignments, she could feel the energy radiating from Jesse as he leaned too close and smiled too often. Thankfully Dr. Hoffman dismissed the class early. As the rest of the class rose to leave, Callie put her hand on Jesse's arm, indicating that he needed to stay in his seat. He would have been pleased to know that his presence was disrupting her thoughts and unsettling her nerves.

"Jesse, what are you doing in this class?"

"Whoa, Callie!" He threw up his hand as though trying to slow down a speeding car in a school zone. "I'm glad to see you, too!" That remark was emphasized as he touched her left hand.

He had her totally off balance and she was impatient for some logic to his presence in the newly offered class. "Yeah, me, too, but what are you doing in this class?"

"Well, for your information, I'm leaning towards a major in criminal justice now and my advisor encouraged me to pick up this new class. Knowing you were taking it didn't hurt. Callie, you know how much I enjoy the old cowboy movies and all those Simon and Simon and Rockford Files shows. Don't you think this will be an exciting class?" Before she could answer him, he added, "Getting to be your partner again is an unexpected bonus."

She rolled her eyes. "I've heard you talk about all those detective shows, but I had no idea you were considering a career in criminal justice. You don't seem the type."

"Well, that's an area of my life you will soon discover, Callie Dear."

"Jesse Collins, I am not your Dear!"

"O my! Touchy, aren't we?" With a smile that would slay half of the female population on the campus, he corrected her, "I didn't refer to you as *my* dear. Not that I wouldn't like to, but disappointingly it seems you aren't ready for that yet."

"You are right. I'm not." Callie was aware she was being short and semi-rude, but she seemed powerless to respond differently. While she welcomed the adventure he offered, the relationship scared her.

"Gee, Callie, I'm glad you are in such a congenial mood. Don't forget. We'll be working cases together." He stood up and collected his belongings. "Our brief rendezvous hints of a very interesting semester."

With his free hand he began to dramatically rub and massage his right knee and then his hip. "Yep, it's going to be a challenging class. I can feel it in my bones, and all of a sudden they're aching something fierce." And with that he bent over and hobbled out of the classroom like a ninety year old man. The professor watched him with much empathy ... until he saw Callie laughing. *It's hard not to like Jesse, even if his behavior is sometimes bizarre.*

In addition to her Jesse encounter and the chaotic emotional aftermath, Callie had a full day of classes. By evening she was weary and ready for a break. After dropping off her books at the dorm, she headed for the cafeteria to meet Heather who had mentioned inviting a new student and his roommate to meet them for supper.

They went through the line, found an empty table for four and began digging into their food. Callie caught a glimpse of bodies moving in their direction from her left. She couldn't believe her eyes. Jesse and some guy she had never seen before plopped their trays on the table. Surely this was not the new student and his roommate -- but oh contraire -- it was. Jesse must be the other roommate. *Does he have built-in radar?*

"Hey, Callie," Jesse boomed. "I didn't realize that my new roommate was talking about your Heather when he invited me to eat with his new friend and her roomie." He must have read the disbelief in Callie's eyes. "Scout's honor," he said giving her the traditional Boy Scout salute. "This was not planned ... but I am not complaining. In fact, I'm rather intrigued by the events of this day. Quite miraculous, don't you think?"

Callie's sigh hinted of surrender. "I'm leaning more towards bewildering. I'm wondering if there are any more inconceivable events in store today. After all, there's six hours left." Her eyes scanned his body. "I see your aching bones have improved."

"Now Callie, you can't blame the events of this day on me. It's God, fate or luck. I opt for God myself. I'll let you reach your own conclusion." He paused and chuckled. "My bones? Another miracle, it seems."

"Well, since I don't believe in fate or luck, that narrows it down to God and I'm struggling with His intent." She studied his gorgeous face and in the process was subdued by his riveting smile. "And you really ought to be ashamed of yourself. That gullible professor felt sorry for you ... and your aching bones."

He winked at Callie and with a mischievous gleam in his eyes turned his attention to Heather. "I see you've already met my new roommate, Heather. Have I ever told you how much I like *your* roomie? Thanks for asking Kirk and me to join you."

Heather and Kirk inquired about their bantering and were intrigued by the events of the day. Before long all four were laughing and enjoying friends -- old and new.

Callie learned that Kirk was a transfer from a junior college who had been recruited for the football team which explained his being Jesse's roommate. Heather seemed rather interested. He could have been Hoss Cartwright's brother. He was a giant of a man physically but had a gentleness and warmth that made a woman feel protected and safe. Callie liked him.

The foursome shared many evening meals after that day. Jesse and Callie settled into being case study partners.

A couple of weeks later, in the middle of discussing their current case study, Jesse interrupted. "Hey, Cal. Would you consider mixing school with personal … as in dating your study partner?"

She laid down her pen and looked at him. "What kind of date, Jesse?"

"There's an ice hockey game next Sunday. We can go alone or we can invite Kirk and Heather to join us."

"If Kirk and Heather agree to join us, I'm game."

"Then we have a date. I've already asked and they've already agreed. Be ready about 5:00 -- that would be p.m. We'll stop for dinner along the way and then head for the arena. Have you ever been to an ice hockey game?"

"No, that's one sport I've not watched or played. I hear it's fun." And as though never interrupted, Callie turned her focus back to the case study.

*How does she do that?* Jesse's heart was mimicking the drums again and his feet began tapping out the beat. Callie looked at him and then peeked under the table. "Nervous feet, Jess?"

"No. Happy feet." He needed to ask his folks if he had any Native American blood in his veins. This was becoming common place around Callie.

Jesse wondered how his list queen would react if she knew she had moved up five notches on the criteria list. He tried to focus on the case notes, but his heart and feet kept overriding his brain functions. Sunday couldn't come soon enough for Jesse.

To his delight, the ice hockey event delivered a great first date. The foursome were incredibility compatible and it actually felt more like friends together than dates. Jesse knew not to push Callie. They held hands a time or two, but mostly -- they just had fun being together as more than study partners.

The next time Jesse went home he told his parents about Callie's thirteen checkmarks on his list and briefly shared his interest in her. He mentioned her previous engagement to David as the delay to his plans. They advised him to take it easy. "Sorry, folks. My heart ignores facts where she is concerned."

Two weeks after their first date, Jesse ask her out again. He invited Kirk and Heather to meet them at the local bowling alley. To Jesse's delight and surprise, Callie was a better than average bowler. In fact, she and Kirk were in a friendly competition. Jesse decided to honor the king and queen of the lanes that night by making paper crowns out of an old advertisement he found. Of course, he insisted they wear them. And before the evening was over, Jesse was bowing every time either of them made a strike.

It was another great date. Jesse was ecstatic. Callie was a good sport and wore the silly crown. He hoped her enjoyment outweighed any embarrassment he caused. He liked to see folks happy.

# Chapter 29

The more time Callie spent with Jesse and the more she talked to David, the weightier her guilt and the greater her confusion. *I know I love David. Why am I so drawn to Jesse? Is that natural?* Those thoughts and questions kept the adventure and her freedom from being all she thought it would be.

David called Sunday afternoon. She listened as he shared about the challenges and blessings of working with his dad and the enjoyment of being out of school. "Dad and I are having some profitable conversations that I wish we'd had a few years ago, Callie. It would have saved you and me a heap of grief. And just so you know -- I'm still not dating."

She didn't have the heart to tell him she was dating.

"Callie, are you and Jesse dating?"

Her silence shouted the answer.

"I have no right to say a word and no one to blame but myself."

She agreed but didn't say so.

David ended the conversation. "I love you. Guess I'd better let you go."

She heard the click and felt his sadness and pain. *I love him, but I'm hurting him. He loved me, but hurt me. What kind of love does that?*

Jesse knew something had upset Callie when she walked into class Monday morning. He didn't need Sherlock to figure out it probably had something to do with David. He walked her to the library after class. They needed more information before wrapping up their last case.

"David called last night." She offered without looking his way.

"What's going on with him?" He was studying her body language.

Callie glanced his way as they made their way to their study spot. "He's doing well. He told me he wasn't dating and when I didn't respond, he asked if we were dating. He wasn't angry with me, but he was deeply hurt." She took a deep breath as though she shared his pain. "What am I going to do? I still love him, but I also know that I have feelings for you. What is wrong with me, Jesse?"

"Wrong with you? Hurt him? Callie, that jerk played around with another girl on and off for three years while you were wearing his ring and avoiding me. And now you tell me he is hurt because we are dating? I personally don't give a rip if he's hurting. I witnessed the pain he inflicted on you, remember?" He hesitated, but decided to say it all. "Still love him? Excuse me for being blunt, I don't understand a love like his that would betray and lie to you and I sure don't comprehend a love like yours that overlooks his sorry excuses."

Callie's mouth dropped open, but it was the shocked expression on her face that changed his direction. Realizing he may have said too much, with a sad and almost rejected expression, he asked, "Do you want me out of your life, Callie?"

She had asked herself that question just recently. "No, and even if I did, God seems determined to throw us together, but if you choose to walk away from me, I'll understand. I know I've complicated your life, Jesse. I'm sorry."

His transformation from anger to rejection to a calm confidence was like watching an emotional chameleon. "Good. I was wondering if you would go home with me this weekend. My family wants to meet you."

"Exactly what have you told them, Jesse?"

"Nothing for you to fret about. They know we are friends and I like you."

She relaxed some with that statement. "Tell me more about your family."

"Well, I've already told you there are eight of us. Mom and Dad. That would be Margaret and Dean to you. Then there's Roger, Chet, Will, Brad and Lizzie."

"You're the oldest. How old is Lizzie?"

"Yep. Lizzie just turned seven. No telling how many more of us there would be if Mom hadn't had Lizzie. She was determined to have a girl. Mom and Dad came from big families and agreed the benefits outweigh the challenges, so mom birthed a new Collins every eighteen to thirty months. Life is never boring. Didn't you tell me you enjoy riding horses? We have several."

"I'd love to go riding. When do we leave and what should I pack?"

"I'll pick you up around 5:00, Friday evening. Pack jeans, a couple of warm tops and a jacket. Better add some good dancing shoes and riding boots."

Callie was ready when Jesse showed up Friday. She met him in the lobby, travel bag in her hand. Jesse was excited. Callie was curious.

# Chapter 30

Callie hadn't seen much of Oklahoma outside of Norman her first two years at OU. The flatter terrain was quite a contrast to the hills and mountains of Virginia and helped explained why this area was ranked third in the number of tornados per year, only behind Texas and Kansas. She had witnessed her share of rough storms during her time here, but nothing catastrophic.

She looked at Jesse. "Have your folks lived here long?"

"Yeah, Dad's great grandfather acquired the first one hundred and sixty acres through the Land Run of 1889. Other acreage has been purchased through the years and it's now a good size ranch for this area. The South Canadian River forms one of our boundaries."

"Your dad grew up here?"

"Yeah, and his dad as well. He's never known any other place as home. It's a good place to raise a big family. I'm not cut out to be a rancher, but Roger and Brad never want to leave. That pleases Dad."

"Wow! That's interesting stuff. I'm looking forward to a relaxing weekend on your historic ranch."

"I'm looking forward to a relaxing weekend with you, *Sweetheart.*" He reached for her hand.

"Now, Jesse, you know I'm not …"

"Oh, I know you're not my sweetheart yet, but *Honey*, I sure am working on it." He was holding tight to her hand as she attempted to pull it away.

"Jesse! Don't you start that kind of talk around your folks! You hear me?"

"Yes, *Darling*! You are coming through loud and clear." He lifted her hand to his lips and kissed it.

She jerked it away and looked out the side window. "I may have to get one of your brothers to drive me back to school first thing in the morning if you keep this up."

He chuckled. "You can try, *Babe*, but I don't think you'll have much success. I've already threatened their lives if they get within six feet of you. My brothers happen to like pretty girls and I had to stake my claim and set up the boundaries before you arrived. Six feet all weekend."

A sigh of surrender said it all. "You are not going to behave, are you?"

"Never fear. My folks will make sure I toe the line, but their definition and yours varies. Trust me, *Dear*. You have nothing to fear. My family already likes you."

That got her attention. "How can they already like me? I thought you just told them we were friends."

"Well, I might have said a little more than that. I'm pretty sure I told them you are my reigning list queen. How could they not like you?"

Callie was getting ready to get out of his truck, but with that last statement, she stared at him. "You didn't!" He wasn't staring. He was admiring the view ... and she was pretty sure she knew what was on his mind.

She looked away, trying to grab hold of her heart that kept gravitating to the masterpiece sitting beside her. Then without a word, she exited the truck and began walking toward the house. She needed some distance between them. She actually had thoughts of kissing him. And she was confident his thoughts were on the same track.

Joining those reflections was an interesting awareness. David's betrayal had made her feel insufficient as a woman. Jesse was a shot in the arm to her femininity. He was her ego booster. Surely that was not the basis of her feelings for him. That would be unfair to everyone, especially Jesse. She needed to sleep on that selfish possibility.

Jesse ran after her, grabbed her arm and swung her around to face him. "Hold up, Callie. You need to be properly introduced before you go mingling with this bunch." He was still wearing that same admiring look and his eyes were staring at her lips. He was going to kiss her!

About that time a loud commotion came from a rather large barn as seven people of assorted sizes started moving towards them. Suddenly she was surrounded by four brothers that definitely came from the same gene pool. And tucked between all those male offspring was a darling seven year old tomboy with pigtails hanging halfway down her back and a smile and dimples that matched Jesse's. He swung her in the air and hugged her warmly before putting her down.

He put his arm around Callie and introduced his mom and dad. So the piercing blues and curly blonde originated with Margaret and those chiseled faces – dimples included -- were copies of Dean's. What a combination!

Then in order from oldest to youngest, he introduced the boys and then Lizzie. Each brother stepped forward, offered her a hand, and then as if mentally measuring, backed about six feet away. Lizzie stayed close. Callie looked at Jesse and then at the brothers and everybody broke out in collective, heartwarming laughter.

Jesse reclaimed his girl by again placing his arm around her and pulling her close. "I wasn't kidding you, Callie. They've been given their warnings -- fair and square -- six feet!"

Roger, who looked to be only a year or two younger than Jesse, spoke up. He was a mixture of charm and mischief that found expression in his engaging smile!

"Yeah, we've had our warning, but that threat will be waived when the square dancing starts tomorrow night. We intend to keep you as far away from *Lover Boy* as possible, so plan on a long night of dancing, *Darling*." He winked at her and waited for a comeback from Jesse.

Strangely and evidently out of character, Jesse didn't say a word. He seemed to be mulling over the situation. After studying Roger and eyeing Callie, he snatched her hand and began to drag her towards his truck.

"What do you think you are doing, Jesse?" she asked as she dug her heels into the dirt.

"First they interrupted my kiss and now this. I don't figure to share you with that crew plus all the other cowboys that will be showing up at that dance. He's right. They could keep you from me the entire night. I won't have it, I tell you. I'll just haul you back to school. I wasn't thinking clearly when I invited you for this weekend. Sorry, *Babe*, we just can't stay."

His brothers and sister ran to her rescue. The boys grabbed Jesse while Lizzie seized Callie's hand and led her into the house. Callie looked back to see all four boys, no, make that five on the ground rolling and tumbling like a bunch of feral cats.

Lizzie kept hold of Callie's hand and led her down a long hall into a rather large bedroom. "You don't mind sharing a room with me, do you, Callie?"

This was definitely a princess suite. A private bath, lots of closets, twin beds, a desk and a small sitting area with large windows that offered a panoramic view of the back property of the ranch left no doubt that Lizzie was prized. "I'd be honored to share your charming place, Lizzie. Thank you for offering." Callie couldn't shake the scene of the brotherly brawl. "Tell me, do your brothers wrestle like that often?"

"Oh, only about four or five times a day. Mom can't handle more than that."

It was evident the kid wasn't joking. "That few, huh? Does anyone ever get hurt?"

"Nah." Callie's questioning expression must have prompted a more honest answer. "Well, at least not real bad. There was this one time when Brad broke his arm. He climbed up kind of high in a tree to hide ... and then tried to jump on Roger as he was walking by. He missed Roger and hit the ground ... hard. Mama outlawed jumping out of high trees after that."

If that wasn't considered serious, Callie decided she didn't want to hear about the others, so she changed directions. "Do you have girlfriends over to play, Lizzie?"

"Sure do, but even then females around here are always outnumbered, except among the cattle. Mama says she's looking forward to her sons marrying someday, so she'll have more daughters. That's why everyone is so pleased Jesse brought you home. I overheard him talking to Mama and Daddy about you. Since he's never brought a girl home before, they figured he must be pretty serious. Has he ever told you about his list?"

Callie nodded.

"Well, I heard him calling you his list queen and that got Mama thinking about wedding bells and a new daughter. Is she right, Callie? I sure would like to have you for a sister."

Callie was speechless. She came here for adventure and to see what it would be like to date someone else and within the first hour there was talk of wedding bells? *This was not what I had in mind.*

Lizzie grabbed her hand and headed out the door.

"Hey, where are you taking my girl, Lizzie?" Jesse inquired while brushing the dirt off his clothing.

Callie sent him a disapproving glance. "Excuse me, family. I've just had a sweet reminder that she is not *my* girl. Nothing serious going on between us. Let me reintroduce you to my friend, *not my girlfriend*, Callie."

Seven of the Collins clan took turns looking at each other, then with seven different *who is he kidding* expressions, broke out into hoots and hollers that reminded her of a rodeo crowd! She wasn't accustomed to all this testosterone. Jesse shrugged his shoulders and gave her one of those *I tried to tell you* looks and went to the truck to get their luggage.

After supper they gathered to play games. Jesse's family knew how to be together and have fun. They consumed dishpans of popcorn and peanuts. By the time they called it quits, the family room looked like an Oklahoma twister had touched down. Callie was pleasantly surprised when everyone pitched in as she and Margaret began to cleanup. In no time, order was restored and the crowd disappeared into the roomy ranch house for the night.

The next morning Dean encouraged Jesse to saddle a couple of horses and show Callie the ranch. She invited Lizzie to join them. Delight filled Lizzie's eyes as Jesse placed her on his horse. "Think we need a chaperone, do you?" Jesse asked with yesterday's intentions still evident in his eyes. She smiled and mounted a beautiful golden Palomino.

The day passed quickly and soon the family headed to the dance. True to their word, his brothers and the other cowboys kept a wide perimeter around Callie and Jesse was not allowed in. Everyone, but Jesse, was enjoying Roger's prank.

Callie had always enjoyed square dancing and a couple of the guys were teaching her some new dances. They made it a point to inform Jesse how much fun they were having.

While dancing with Roger she questioned him about a girlfriend. "Not tonight. Had to find out if my brother was sticking to his list and also pay him back for a few pranks he's played on me and some of my dates. You have any sisters?"

"Yeah, but she's fourteen. Roger, you've lined up every male here to dance at least one dance with me. I can't even get my breath. Why don't you encourage Jesse to dance with some of the girls, especially the one sitting beside him that keeps staring at us? Is she your girlfriend?"

"I'll get to her later. Right now I'm checking out a potential Collins addition."

Callie wondered if he was going to pry her mouth open and check out her teeth. Relief came when someone else grabbed her for the next dance. First Lizzie and now Roger. Evidently bringing a girl home was nothing to sneeze at in the Collins household. She wished she had known that family tidbit before signing on for the weekend. Adventure and curiosity were taking on new meanings.

Jesse was not his usual, jovial self when the evening festivities concluded. They rode home with a couple of his younger brothers. He reached for her hand, intertwined their fingers and held on tight. When they arrived home, he held her back. After the others headed for the house, he nudged her towards the barn. Following his lead, she began to brush the horse she had ridden that morning.

"Jess, Roger and the others were just having some fun tonight. Nothing happened."

"Yeah, I know. I'm usually in the middle of such shenanigans, but tonight I learned that being on the other end is not nearly as much fun."

He turned his attention from his horse to her. "Tonight just made me more of aware of my real problem."

"Well, that sounds serious, Jesse."

"Oh, it's serious, alright." He moved away from the horse and grabbed her closest hand. His brilliant blue eyes were searching her soft orbs of brown. "You see, Cal, I've fallen in love with my list queen, but I'm not sure how she feels about me."

She was not ready for that bit of information. She stared at him as the words echoed inside her head and tugged at her heart. *What have I done?*

When she didn't respond, he continued. "First, you were engaged and then you weren't. Only then did I feel like I had a fighting chance. That's why I wanted you and my folks to meet. I want a future with you, Callie.

"I was excited about showing you off to my home town buddies, but I sure didn't plan on them dancing the night away with you while I sat on the sidelines. I'm still considering punching Roger's lights out."

She wanted to tell him that he didn't need to fret about Roger. He was just checking out a possible family acquisition, but opted for silence.

When she didn't respond, he turned on the radio which was set to a country-western station and reached for her other hand. A new Kenny Rogers song was playing. "Dance with me, Callie."

She hesitated.

"Please."

She slowly reached for his offered hand as he placed his other hand above her waist and began to move her to the rhythm of the music. He began to harmonize with Kenny. A Glenn Campbell sounding voice ... and a smooth dancer. The attraction was getting stronger. She stopped and studied the appealing cowboy. *This hunk is offering me his heart and mine belongs to someone else.* The depth of his feelings shocked her ... and made her feel guilty.

"Callie, I love you." His eyes moved to her lips. At first he kissed her gently and she felt her knees go weak. Just as she was catching her breath, he kissed her again, but this was no light brush of the lips. He was announcing his love and seeking hers. Major butterfly alert! And wild horses on the horizon. "I've wanted to do that for over a year, Lab Partner."

Whoa! He was not playing around -- anymore. *If my heart wasn't already taken, I could be persuaded!* She stepped out of his reach. "Jesse, you are one of the two neatest guys in all the world and I like you -- a lot, but my heart belongs to David." Shocked by her response to his kiss, she slowly backed away from him and disappeared into the night.

As she entered Lizzie's room, Callie was aware that the barn wasn't the only place in need of mucking. Jesse's declaration of love and that kiss uncovered her camouflaged self-centeredness in their relationship. He had been open and honest from the beginning. Though she had admitted her love for David, she had also played with Jesse's heart while waiting for hers to heal. *Love? Do I even know what the word means?*

She remembered the passage from I Corinthians 13 that describes love. Grateful that Lizzie was asleep, she found the Amplified Version. That would help. She read that passage several times trying to understand what it was saying and where she was missing it.

*1 Corinthians 13:4-8[4] Love endures long and is patient and kind; love never is envious nor boils over with jealousy, is not boastful or vainglorious, does not display itself haughtily.[5] It is not conceited (arrogant and inflated with pride); it is not rude (unmannerly) and does not act unbecomingly. Love (God's love in us) does not insist on its own rights or its own way, for it is not self-seeking; it is not touchy or fretful or resentful; it takes no account of the evil done to it [it pays no attention to a suffered wrong].[6] It does not rejoice at injustice and unrighteousness, but rejoices when right and truth prevail.[7] Love bears up under anything and everything that comes, is ever ready to believe the best of every person, its hopes are fadeless under all circumstances, and it endures everything [without weakening].[8] Love never fails [never fades out or becomes obsolete or comes to an end].*

That was revealing and convicting. Not self-seeking. Focuses on others. *Selfish and unselfish love.* Callie knew which pond she had been splashing in lately.

She made no attempt to see Jesse after the barn scene. She had some serious confessing and thinking to do.

Jesse stayed in the barn. He was crushed. *She's still hung up on the creep who betrayed her.* Mucking stalls seemed appropriate for his current mood, and the horses didn't walk away when he poured out his heart.

*What happened to falling in love and living happily ever after? Just fairy tales or some writer's romantic fantasy? I'm beginning to wonder.*

Jesse slept a couple of hours, showered and went back to the barn. His family seemed to understand that something unexpected had occurred last night. It was an unusually quiet morning among the Collins crew -- for the time being. Knowing his family and their track record, it wouldn't last long. It's hard to keep a secret in a big family. Somebody's bound to find out and then it's public record.

He saw Roger and Callie coming his direction. There wasn't much time before church, but he wanted to talk to her alone -- if possible. "Morning, Callie."

"Morning, Jesse."

"Mighty clean barn, Bro. Late night?" Roger teased as he headed for the tack room.

Callie moved close to Jesse. "Jesse. I'm not upset with you. Actually I'm upset with myself."

"Callie, am I only a friend to you?"

"Oh, Jesse, you are much more than a friend and that is my problem. Your kiss proved that. Why do you think I walked away?"

"So I'm not a zero in your book?"

"A Zero? Far from it! Zeroes don't have that effect on me. Jesse Collins, you're a hundred and ten … without question."

His mesmerizing smile lit up his face as he reached for her. She put out a hand to stop him.

"Problem is that another hundred and ten man has already claimed my heart. If it wasn't for David, we would be having a different conversation right now. I can't walk away from him. Jess," With a new awareness of the pain her self-centeredness was going to inflict, she added, "I never meant for you to love me."

He crashed through the invisible barrier she was trying to establish and pulled her close. "Callie, you knew about my list. You knew I didn't date casually. You knew you were my list queen. How could you not know I was falling in love with you?"

She pushed away from his embrace. "I guess I didn't want to accept that fact. When David hurt me, I wanted someone to make me feel attractive and desirable. You did that. You're right. I knew about your list. I've used you, Jesse. I'm sorry." She turned and rushed towards the house.

"Trouble in paradise, Lover Boy?" Roger asked on his way back to the house.

"Not now, Roger. Not now."

Jesse stayed in the barn so long that Margaret came out to check on him. "Son, you're going to be late for church if you don't hurry."

"Callie and I are headed back to school, Mom. We won't make church this morning. And please don't ask why."

Jesse followed his mom back into the house and knocked on Lizzie's door. "Cal, get your bag packed. We are heading back to school when the family leaves for church."

Things got very quiet in the Collins hacienda the next fifteen minutes. When Callie walked out with her bag, Jesse was already at the door with his.

Callie tried to be gracious and grateful under strained circumstances. Margaret turned to her son. "Jesse, can't you two stay until this afternoon. I've cooked your favorite beef barbeque."

"It's best we leave now, Mom."

Callie followed him out the door and headed for his truck while Jesse cornered Roger.

Neither Jesse nor Callie said a word the first thirty or forty miles. Jesse finally broke the silence. "Callie, I think I get it. You're afraid you will love me so now you are going to put distance between us, aren't you?" She didn't respond.

"As disappointed as I am about this weekend, I'm not giving up on us," Jesse warned.

"Oh, Jesse, I've complicated life for all three of us. And yes, I'm backing off until this thing between David and me is resolved."

"What do you mean by resolved?"

"Jesse, David hasn't dated since we broke up. He has demonstrated a genuine godly sorrow about his wrong choices from the beginning. He wants to reconcile and get married. I've been the hold up."

"Are you telling me that all of a sudden you trust him again?"

"It's not been sudden, Jesse, but yes, I do trust him."

His anger surfaced again. "Callie, I don't get it! Why would you risk trusting a low-down, two-timer again?"

"I don't know how to explain it; I just do."

"Well, then you should understand my problem. I love you and I can't explain that either. Considering the one-sided relationship we've had, it makes no more sense than you still loving David."

They were quiet the rest of the trip.

They had a few weeks of classes left together which meant she couldn't close him out.

Jesse shared with Heather and she encouraged him to hang tight. "She cares more for you than she admits, Jesse. I think that has scared her."

"Well, I can tell you that her response has scared me, but I'm not giving up unless his ring goes back on her finger."

# Chapter 31

The semester was over. Without Callie's knowledge, Jesse arranged with Heather to drive Callie to the airport before he headed home. He was not giving up … not yet. Callie was surprised but not upset. They chatted about family and the upcoming bowl game, but he didn't set this up for small talk. "Are you going to date David again, Callie?"

"If he asks."

That answer shook the foundation of his vacillating confidence. "Oh, he'll ask. Are you going to tell him about me? And us?"

"About you? Yes. But Jesse, there-is-no-us. I've been wrong and selfish to allow you to think that."

"Callie, I refuse to believe that getting involved with me was wrong. You weren't being selfish. You had been hurt. Why wouldn't you want to be with someone who loved you and wasn't going to hurt you? I make you a promise, Callie Adams, your number two man will not betray you like your number one man has."

She studied the funny, energetic and sweet man sitting beside her. She wondered how he would respond if someone like Josie was on his trail, but she kept her thoughts to herself.

He parked and unloaded her suitcase. As they walked, he reached for her free hand. She pondered his last comment.

When they arrived at her departure gate, he pulled her to a less congested area. He kissed her forehead and then waited until her eyes met his. "I love you, my list queen. Don't forget that while you're away."

Hearing his repeated confession of love and title of endearment triggered tears of regret. Callie withdrew and sat in a nearby seat.

Jesse moved beside her. "Callie, I don't ever mean to make you cry. My desire is to see you smile."

Callie looked past the arctic blues into his heart and knew he had spoken truth. "Of all the girls in your life, why did you have to fall for me?"

"Cupid pierced my heart the day we met and since then it's had a mind of its own where you are concerned. It would have been easier to change the course of one of your mountain streams than the path my heart was determined to take with you. I couldn't stop it and you couldn't have prevented it."

He brushed back a stray curl and waited until her eyes met his. Ignoring those around them, he kissed her before helping her up. "Don't forget to watch our game Christmas day. I'll be playing for you, Callie."

"Are your folks going to the game?"

"Dad and Roger plan to be there. I had hoped you could join them."

"I'll watch, Jesse." She backed away and then turned to join the other passengers making their way to the plane.

Jesse understood about the thrill of victory and the agony of defeat ... especially in football, but regarding matters of the heart ... that was a new playing field. Regarding the latter he had done his best, but he was determined to approach the Fiesta Bowl as though he were playing for Callie's heart. He had to win.

# Chapter 32

John met Callie at the airport and she could hardly wait to get home. She quickly unpacked, called David's work place and left a message. Before she could walk out of the room, he called back. She had been both eager and anxious about their meeting since Jesse's confession.

David seemed as glad to hear her voice as she was his. "Do you have plans for lunch, David?"

"None that can't be changed. What do you have in mind?"

"Someplace we can talk privately."

"We could have a winter picnic. I know it sounds weird, but the push to conserve energy by using our natural resources has hit our city planners. They have installed some large glass panels in a couple of the pavilions at the city park. Amazingly enough, on days like this one, they are rather comfortable. I can reserve one if you are interested."

"Sounds great!"

He made arrangements to pick her up. A couple of hours later, she pulled back her curtain when she heard a vehicle pull into the driveway. David was exiting a new Mulsanne blue Corvette. She stared. Not only was the car spectacular, the man getting out wasn't lacking either. Maybe it was the absence. Maybe it was trust restored. Maybe it was a boy becoming a man. Whatever it was propelled her down the stairs.

"I've got the door, Mom." She opened it before he knocked and knew she was looking at the man she wanted to marry. Looking past him, she admired his new wheels. "Quite a car you have there."

"Thought you might like it." Had he ordered it with her in mind? She had made no secret of her fondness for the classy cars with an attitude. She walked past him … admiring its sleek lines and wondering what it would be like to drive it. He opened the driver's door and handed her the keys.

"Are you serious?" He nodded and moved to the passenger side. David had her stop at a local diner where he picked up a couple of box lunches. Most of the conversation during the ride centered on the car and her questions about his life since graduation.

As predicted, the enclosed pavilion was cozy warm. Both knew the food was an excuse to be together, but neither was confident enough to approach the barrier that stood between them.

They tried for small talk, but both were primed to move on. David paved the way. "As devastating as our breakup has been, God has used it as a purging and refining time in my life. I still marvel at the power of forgiveness -- from God, you and now myself."

"Is that the difference in you? You remind me of the David I used to know, but there's an added dimension I can't put my finger on. What's going on?"

"Going on?" He chuckled. "Let's see. I'm glad to be out of school and working with Dad. God's mercies are new every morning. And it's good to see you after four months. How about you?"

"Me? I've missed you, David Henderson."

"You have?" He breathed a noticeable sigh of relief and took her hands in his. "How about the trust issue?"

"I trust you, David. It's no longer a problem."

The release that flooded him inwardly was visible outwardly. He scooted close and laced his fingers with hers.

"One more question. This one has tested my faith regarding God's plans for my life. Has dating Jesse caused you to question your love for me?"

"David, dating Jesse has complicated my life." *No more secrets.* "Jesse cares for me."

David dropped her hands and put some space between them. "Do you care for him?"

"Yes, but my feelings for him are different than my love for you."

"If it wasn't for Jesse, would you be struggling with our relationship?"

"No. If Jesse wasn't in my life, I think you and I would definitely be engaged. I also think if you weren't in my life that I could love him, but you are in my life ... and in my heart. He hasn't lessened my love for you, but he has made me aware than I could care for someone else."

He paced. He watched a couple of playful squirrels gathering hickory nuts. Then he turned to face her.

"You were young when we started dating. I had dated a few other girls but found none touched my heart as you already had. I've considered dating since we broke up, but the truth is -- I'm not going anywhere until you tell me there is no chance for us."

That was her open door. "Well, Mr. Henderson, your chances have greatly increased. The shutout is over."

She heard his quick intake of breath. He stilled. His eyes questioning. His pointer finger waving between them. "You mean dating? You and me?"

She nodded.

He pulled her to her feet as latent joy erupted into laughter and lit up his eyes. He swept her into his arms. "Welcome home, Callie." She laid her head on his shoulder and agreed. The silence that followed was healing.

"I have an idea for the first date. We can make up for the ones we've missed by having a cuddling and smooching marathon -- beginning now."

She pushed him away with a playful shove, ran to his car and locked the doors. He slowly strolled her way, dangling the keys and wearing a Rhett Butler smile. He unlocked her door. "Okay, what turned you off? The marathon part or the now part? I'm willing to negotiate."

"Actually, I'm considering reinstating the shutout."

"Too late! And I won't give you reason for another one." He reached for her hand and gently guided her out of the car. "Let's clean up and I'll let you drive our new car anywhere you want to go today."

"Now that's a deal and a date!" They spent the rest of the day visiting favorite scenic spots along the Blue Ridge Parkway and catching up. He didn't make any further attempts to kiss her -- that day or the ones that followed. He had put her through much and he was giving her time. After all Jesse was still in the picture.

# Chapter 33

Their next outing, David placed the heart necklace in her hands. As she lifted it in place, he swept aside her hair, fastened the clasp and lightly kissed her neck. "I see you're still wearing the ID bracelet."

"I've never taken it off, Callie. It's a treasured gift."

They didn't have to plan dates. The events of the season did that and kept them busy and together most of the time. Joseph was so delighted they were dating again that he gave David as much time off work as he needed.

They spent time with her family and Callie joined David and Joseph for a couple of nostalgic cooking evenings. It was like old times -- but better.

Christmas day, Callie and her dad were watching the Sooners play the Wyoming Cowboys in the Fiesta Bowl. David and Joseph were scheduled to join the family for dinner and fellowship. The time for their arrival was nearing. "Dad, you're not going to leave that on when David and Uncle Joseph arrive, are you?"

"Of course not, but have you noticed that Jesse is playing one of his best games?"

She could only nod. Tears were close.

"It's been hard for you to watch him, hasn't it?"

"You have no idea. Dad, he's the second greatest guy I've ever met. My selfishness is going to crush him."

"Learn from your experiences, Callie. Hopefully Jesse will, too."

"I pray you are right."

The Henderson men arrived and John turned off the game. The families enjoyed an evening filled with many of the traditions of the season, including a table filled with a baked Virginia ham, homemade yeast rolls, candied sweet potatoes, seven layered salad, and sweet garden peas with pearl onions. A homemade carrot cake finished off the menu. Eggnog and wassail were always available.

After the meal, David and Callie found a quiet corner and exchanged gifts. David had chosen a gold, braided three strand bracelet for Callie. His card referenced Ecclesiastes 4:12. *A cord of three strands is not quickly torn apart.* He slipped the bracelet over her right hand.

"I'm learning to value physical reminders of spiritual truths. Thank you for this one."

Callie had arranged with Joseph to select some of David's favorite pictures of Ella. With the help of her mom's artistic gifting and her dad's wood working skills, they had tastefully designed and framed a lovely collection of small photos into one larger display. David was not only surprised, he was moved -- by the gift and the givers. A few tears were shed as they remembered Ella.

As was the tradition, John read Luke's telling of the familiar Christmas story. This night, Callie made the connection between the unselfish love of I Corinthians 13 and the babe in the manger. God so loved us that He gave and Jesus so loved us that He came. Jesus was and is Love with skin on. *Now I know what unselfish love lived out looks like. Jesus.*

She looked at David and knew she had loved him conditionally and selfishly since his confession. Life had been more about her since then. No wonder her life was a mess.

When she found a suitable time, she pulled him aside, shared her heart and asked his forgiveness. David's lessons in forgiveness went deep. He reached for her right hand and fingered her new bracelet. "His way this time, Callie."

As the days passed, David was reminded again of the words of Solomon. *Their vineyard of love was once again in full bloom.* God had restored what the foxes had destroyed. His heart was full.

# Chapter 34

David and Callie were headed to a New Year's Eve celebration sponsored by one of the local congregations. Becoming a couple again this holiday season had inspired some inquiring conversations and triggered some delicate questions.

David was tempted to join the basketball game but thought it wiser to partner with Callie in the Rook tournament. They knocked off a couple of challengers only to be bested by a very serious elderly couple. David was suspicious that subtle clues passed between those two seniors.

They by-passed a couple of serious games of Monopoly but agreed to join the gang playing Charades rather than get involved in the wild and loud crowd playing Pit.

As they suspected, they had to field several comments about their cancelled wedding and deflect some questions about their future. Callie deferred to David whose response was pretty much the same. "Things are working out."

As midnight neared, about half the folks, David and Callie included, left and made their way to the town park for the fireworks display. They mingled with the crowd until the countdown started then David drew her close. "Sweet Callie, we, too, have a chance to flip the calendar and start over." Then with a tenderness birthed from the ashes of loss, David not only claimed her lips, but reclaimed her heart.

Words would have been inadequate and were unnecessary. The resurrection of their love was something that could only be understood by the two who had experienced its demise. The skies bore a striking resemblance to the celebration of their hearts. They lingered until the heavens were quiet and their souls were peaceful.

As they neared his car, David hesitated as he reached to open her door. Instead, he reached in his pocket and pulled out Ella's ring. "First things first. Callie, the first time I put this ring on your finger, my affection for you was a blend of unselfish and very self-centered love. And the longer we were engaged, the more self-focused I became. I saw *you* as the one who could and should meet my needs and fulfill my desires. I not only lost sight of you and your needs, I allowed my own to dominate my body and soul and override my love for you. Both of us have experienced the devastation and fallout of that kind of love.

"Tonight this ring comes with a better understanding of love. Out of the ashes and consequences of my selfishness, God keeps revealing His transforming, unselfish love. I know my embryonic understanding is like raindrops compared to the ocean of truth it represents, but sometimes I feel like I'm drowning in the droplets.

He paused and brought the ring close to her left hand. "There was a time when I wasn't sure I'd get a second change to ask you this question. Callie Adams, will you marry me?"

Callie nodded as warm tears trailed down her cold cheeks.

He slipped the ring on her finger and pulled her close. "Please don't go back to Norman next week, Callie. Stay here and let's get married."

He was answered by a smile that lit up the night sky. "I've been hoping you'd ask before I had to leave. I'm ready, David."

David threw his hands in the air and shouted so loudly that everyone in the parking lot heard him. "YES! YES! YES!" His arms circled Callie and he began swinging her round and round as laughter ... his and hers ... joined the sounds of the night. Quite unintentionally, he now had the attention of a small audience. "She said YES!" Congratulations were offered by those close-by.

After everyone moved to their own vehicles, David kissed his girl again. "Callie, we are going to celebrate every New Year with fireworks."

"If you don't settle down, we won't need to buy any. I think we need to take our fireworks home."

Their conversation on the way to her house was filled with excitement and plans for the next few days.

"Where are we going to live, David?"

"Actually, that's already been worked out. It's a surprise that will be ready by the time we get back from our honeymoon, I promise."

"I'm guessing you are not going to tell me about the honeymoon either."

He smiled. "Good guess. Pack for warm weather ... and plan for two weeks. That's all you need to know."

As they pulled in her driveway, he left the engine running to ward off the cold, winter air. A light snow had begun to fall. David turned to Callie and reached for the hand that now displayed his mom's ring. "Callie, I'm impressed to share part of my spiritual journey with you. Do you think your folks will mind if you come in a little later?"

"If the porch light flicks on and off, then I'll need to head in. Otherwise, we are okay."

"Before I start, I want you to know that this is my own unique journey and I'm aware that God's ways of reaching each of us are as different and unique as those snowflakes that are falling."

"We've walked different paths the last nine months, David, but I believe both have been leading us to this night and all that lies ahead. I shared my journey Christmas. Now, I'd like to hear yours."

"Cal, the two darkest times in my life were the day Mom died and the night I walked out of the Washington National Airport with your engagement ring in my pocket. One loss was out of my control. The second one was totally my doing. Even though I knew by that time that God had forgiven me, I felt like I had lost everything in my earthly life that mattered. First Mom and then you.

"Over the next days and weeks, I kept asking one simple question. *Where did I go wrong, Lord?* Dad had told me that lust was the fruit of my sin, not the root. I kept asking and seeking and by the time graduation came, I realized that self-centeredness had been the reason for my lack of honesty with you and my moral failures with Josie.

"Knowing that fact and being able to deal with it were two different issues. I confessed it, but I knew that my self-love needed to be replaced with God's unselfish love. But I had no idea how that exchange could take place.

"I had heard many teachings on God's love, but head knowledge does not always parallel life experiences. I needed to experience God's love personally. Oh, I believed in God. I even believed Jesus was His Son and had died for my sins and based on that I had made a public declaration of my faith and tried to live a decent life, but a personal relationship with God ... I didn't have a clue."

Callie perked up. "That's been my question lately, David. How can I tap into God's love? I'm tired of selfish living. It's too painful for the folks I care about, not to mention the backlash."

"Well, I went to the one person I knew who lives it. My dad. He compared God's love for and pursuit of us to my love for and pursuit of you. He pointed out that the difference is that my love was and is tainted with selfishness and God's is not. Comparing the intensity and passion of my pursuit and love for you to God's for me got my attention. Was it possible that God has that level of desire for a relationship with me?"

"That does bring it into our realm of understanding, doesn't it? What else did Uncle Joseph say?"

"Then he asked me an interesting question. 'What is the universal cry of every human heart?'"

Callie's response was quick. "To love and be loved?"

"Most folks agree! Dad reminded me that love involves relationship and intimacy. His next question stirred my heart and challenged my mind. 'Is it possible that we were created to be loved by God and designed for an intimate relationship with Him?'"

Callie was pondering that possibility. "Created to be loved ... by God? Designed for intimacy ... with Him? Us? With all of our junk? Why would He want us? He doesn't need us." She paused. David sat quietly watching Callie as understanding was dawning. "But, David, if that's true ... that means our need and cry for love is part of our spiritual DNA. That opens the door to some far-reaching questions. The first one that comes to my mind is ... how is such a relationship possible?"

"Paul gives us a clue in Ephesians 5, Callie, when he speaks of Christ and the church while discussing marriage. We know that marriage not only embodies love and relationship, but intimacy … a union, a joining where *the two become one.*"

"Us in union with God? That almost sounds irreverent or sacrilegious. Are you saying that our earthly institution of marriage gives insight into what a relationship with God can or should look like?"

David laughed. "You are asking the same questions I asked Dad. The Apostle Paul called it a mystery, so I'd say it's worthy of investigation, wouldn't you? Consider our journey. During our courtship, we spent time getting to know each other. We fell in love and decided we wanted to be in a permanent relationship. We've certainly had our bumps and challenges, but nonetheless, we have made a commitment to marriage … for the second time."

Callie looked at her ring. "The commitment is different this time, isn't it?"

"Indeed, it is." He leaned close and kissed her softly. "You are getting me sidetracked … and yet it is our own experiences that can help us grab hold of some of this. What's next for us, Callie?"

"The wedding and I am so ready!"

David smiled and kissed her again. "You keep sidetracking me and this may take longer than I figured." He placed his thumb on her ring. "Think about all the things that will be included in our wedding."

"That's all I've been doing since you put the ring back on my finger. A week is short notice, but I'm not complaining."

"Have you ever paid much attention to the wedding vows?"

"Probably not like I should have."

"They are traditionally vows to love each other God's way … unselfishly. Unfaithfulness and the divorce rates prove we don't know how to do that. We mean well, but the truth is that *selfish* love can't live up to those *unselfish* vows.

"I understood what Dad was saying up to this point, but I still didn't know how to solve my dilemma. Then he threw me for a loop with his next question. 'What if after your wedding, you and Callie go back to your separate homes and just date once or twice a week?' I told him there was no possibility of that happening. I'm asking you what he asked me. 'Why not?'"

She laughed in a mocking way. "I'd say someone missed the point of getting married."

David laughed quietly. "I think Dad was enjoying this lesson in more ways than one. He posed another question. 'What if later the two of you decided that you would live together and share all of life ... except the marriage bed?' How would you have responded, Callie?"

She was a little embarrassed. "Well, others might not know about our not sharing the marriage bed, but I'd know and I'd wonder what was wrong with me that you weren't interested."

"And you'd have every right to wonder and you know why? Because we have been created and designed by God to desire and enjoy the love expressed and intimacy shared in the marriage bed. The difference in our bodies affirms God's intent. It's part of our physical DNA as male and female. The physical joining is the culmination of the joining of our hearts and minds that took place at our engagement and wedding. It's a coming together of our whole beings. Body, soul and spirit. That's the point of God's guidelines. Lust involves only the physical joining and leaves the soul and spirit in turmoil because we weren't designed for sex apart from unselfish love. That's what makes sex outside of marriage so destructive to both persons.

"And that's the setting God uses as a metaphor for the relationship He desires with us. Why? Because the real us, our spirits, were created to be loved by Him and designed for the intimacy such love births. Anything less is unnatural and will always leave us empty and looking for love in all the wrong places.

"Think about it, Callie. Union, not sexual, in the spirit with God. A coming together. A shutting out. A closing in. A place of personal intimacy. A place of total acceptance and belonging. A place of being naked and unashamed. A place of yielding and surrender. A place of sharing. A place of exchange. A place of loving and being loved ... unconditionally and unselfishly. A place of rest. A place of renewal. A place of new beginnings.

"I personally think the list is endless, because this God of ours is so immense that eternity will undoubtedly be filled with fresh revelations of Him ... continually.

"I've been living in His house, but ignorance kept me out of His place of personal relationship and intimacy. He used my sin to bring me to my spiritual knees where I shut the world out. He used your rejection to shut me in and it was there I learned to be honest and transparent ... to be naked and unashamed before Him. It was there I began to experience His unconditional and unselfish love. He loved me regardless of what I had done or been, Callie. That kind of love is humbling and life changing ... and freeing. I'm finding that as His love both fills and consumes me, I am being changed. And I'm falling in love with Him.

"I Corinthians 13 love begins to make sense. Living in a love relationship with Him releases His love that is filling me to spill over into my relationship with you. Now I understand Dad's wisdom. Relationship, not lust or dishonesty, was the root of my problem. I cannot imagine what taking His love into our marriage will do, Callie, but I'm ready to find out."

"And I'm ready ... to experience intimacy with Him ... and with you, David. I'm reminded that His love made all of this possible. His love prompted the gift of His Son. His Son's love and life opened the doors to the Father's secret places. His Love. Will we ever fully comprehend it?"

"Not this side of eternity, but He keeps giving us clues. The passage that hit me last week was Isaiah 62:5. *As the bridegroom rejoices over his bride, so Your God will rejoice over you.* When I think of you as my bride, the fireworks start again. Comprehending that God has those kinds of thoughts and feelings for me has blown away plenty of old perceptions of Him and given me a feeling of worth and value that I've never known before. I'm now convinced that He is wild about us and that our earth and universe resound day and night with the proof."

Tears were pooling in Callie's eyes. "David, is it possible that all the love songs and stories of all the ages have been and continue to be the cries of our hearts for the One Who is our Perfect Love?"

"I think that is very likely."

Both sat quietly for a few minutes letting the truths and images of the evening root out some false notions and fill in some blanks.

Callie broke the silence. "Our puritanical embarrassment about discussing sex and intimacy has kept us silent and silence has fed our ignorance. In the meanwhile the world continued to pervert and promote sex outside of God's design and purpose to the point that we live in a world of messed up relationships … personally and spiritually. God help us! We wound and hurt each other often unknowingly and unintentionally with our self-centered ways because we expect from each other what only God can be or give."

Suddenly she turned away and looked out into the darkness of the night as a wave of deep sadness settled over her. "David, I feel guilty experiencing this kind of love with you because of the repercussions my selfishness is going to have on Jesse." She turned to face him. "What am I going to do about him?"

"I don't know, but last night, Callie, I surrendered us – you, Jesse and me and our futures to God."

Callie wept new tears for sweet Jesse.

David exited his side and opened her door. "God wastes nothing in our lives, Callie. Somehow He will use this in Jesse's life. We'll both pray for him."

He walked her to the door. "I don't want to leave you tonight, Cal." He pulled her into his arms as the snow began to swirl around them. "Pastor's asleep and your folks would frown on us camping out in the den, so I guess I'd better get home. I'll call early so we can make plans. A small wedding and a honeymoon coming up." He kissed her with the promise of what was to come.

Callie wasn't ready for him to leave yet. "David, before you go, I have to ask one more question. Do you like big families?"

The light reflected in his eyes and she caught his excitement. "Being an only child has convinced me of the merits of large families. First we get married and then the family will come."

Callie looked at her ring and tiptoed to kiss him one last time. "Someday I want to fill our house with little Davids and Callies, but for starters I'd like a little Ella."

"A little Ella. Yes, I'd like that." Reluctantly she opened the door. He kissed her quickly. "Until tomorrow, my love." He closed the door and lingered after she walked inside. He watched as the snow continued to clothe the world in white. He recalled Isaiah 1:18. *Though your sins are as scarlet, they will be as white as snow.* He was overwhelmed by the grace and love of God.

Callie would be his bride within a week. And she wanted a little Ella. *Thank You, Father.*

He remembered Jesse … and prayed.

# Chapter 35

Callie was sitting in their living room trying to process the events that led up to this night. God had answered her prayers -- through David. He had become the conduit of God's love to her. She was created to be in a love relationship with God. She was learning what that meant through her love relationship with David.

She wanted to wake her folks, especially Carla, and share the great news, but decided it could wait until everyone was up. As she sat looking at the ring and bracelet, she wondered how she could explain any of this to Jesse. Just thinking about his pain pierced her heart.

A ringing phone startled her. She looked at her watch. It was after 2:00 a.m. Her heart raced. No one calls with good news this time of the morning.

She began moving toward the phone and was met by Carla and her parents. The females stood back as John answered. His facial expressions alerted them that this was not good news.

As he hung up, he placed a hand on Callie's shoulder. "There has been a bad wreck at one of the main intersections downtown. Someone ran a red light and one of the cars involved was David's. Due to the nature of his injuries he is being taken to the University of Virginia Hospital. His dad is asking you to come as quickly as you can."

Never in her wildest dreams did she imagine anything like this happening. "Oh, God! No!" She whispered. "Not now! Please not now!" She began to cry and pace around the room. "Oh, God! Please don't let him die!" Her voice began to spiral in intensity.

A mixture of crying and begging so shook her dad that he pulled her into his arms. "Callie, you can't lose it. David needs you." That was all she needed to hear. She began to take deep breaths and placed her left hand on her dad's arm. "David just put his ring back on my finger, Daddy. We need to leave quickly." He kissed her on the forehead and nodded in agreement.

What should have been a joyous announcement and time of celebration was overshadowed by fear of the unknown. A flood of conflicting emotions began clashing in each member of the Adams family. David and Callie were engaged and David was …

John told her to pack a change or two of clothes along with anything else she would need for a few days. He told Carla to get dressed and ride with Callie. He and Beth would follow.

As they left the house, Carla wanted to know about the ring. Callie shared. Both cried and both prayed.

The trip was a blur. The snow slowed them down. Callie found herself in a battle between the unknown possibilities and the consideration that nothing touches us that hasn't passed through God's approval. David and she had been experiencing God's life changing love. What in this world and the next was this all about? She vacillated between wanting to scream and question God and trusting that He had everything under control. *You don't sleep, Lord; so you knew. You allowed it.*

The Adams family rushed into the ER and found Joseph sitting in a corner by himself. John walked toward him and two grown men unashamedly hugged and wept. As the men released each other, Joseph reached for Callie. They fell into each other's arms and shared the ache and fear of what was happening behind the closed doors. Finally he spoke. "He's going to need you, Callie. If anyone can help pull him through this, it's you. You have to know that you are the only girl he's ever loved."

She lifted her ring finger. Joseph was visibly shaken. Both were crying. "I love him, Uncle Joseph, and I'm going to be here for him. What have they told you?"

"I know that he was unconscious, but alive when they brought him in and that he has been rushed to surgery with multiple injuries."

"Do you know what happened?"

"Eye witnesses say that another vehicle traveling at a high rate of speed ran the red light, hitting David on the driver's side. The streets were slick. The driver was intoxicated. David's convertible didn't offer him much protection. I never did feel comfortable about that car, but he loved it."

It was a long night and they waited quietly ... and prayerfully. Finally a surgeon came out and called for the Henderson family. Joseph stood and asked the Adams family to join him. He introduced himself and Callie.

The surgeon explained that David had severe organ damage and his spine was severed near his waist. He was paralyzed from the waist down. Medically, they would do everything they could, but they weren't offering much hope.

Severe damage? A very slim chance? Paralyzed? Callie looked at Joseph. The combination of those words describing David knocked the breath out of them. Tears and more tears.

"Oh, Uncle Joseph, what are we going to do?" Callie cried.

"We're going to trust God and pray for His will above all else, Callie, and then we are going to love David through it all."

Callie spent half the morning reliving the hours they had just shared and the other half crying out for mercy. And as reality began to settle in, the age old question raised its head. *WHY GOD? WHY?*

She knew this was no accident with God. Ten or fifteen seconds would have made all the difference. Why did she ask him that last question? Why didn't he kiss her one more time? Why didn't they camp out in the living room until morning? *Why, God? Why?*

Three days passed and still he remained unconscious.

*What good can possibly come out of this tragedy, God? Yes, it's a tragedy! You didn't cause it, but you didn't prevent it.* She was angry. *I know, I know. You are God and I am not, but You are asking too much.* She wanted to scream! She wanted to turn back the clock so she could change the outcome. She wanted to wake up from the nightmare she was experiencing. She wanted God to make it better.

*Daughter, if I AM who I say I AM -- regardless of how it turns out, dare to trust Me.*

Callie calmed as those words began to bring some sanity to her mind and calmness to her emotions. Vividly, some of David's last words of only a few days ago came rushing into her mind and heart. *He surrendered the three of us to Your will, God. And this is Your response?*

David regained consciousness the fourth day and was able to communicate some. He lit up when he saw Callie. She stayed close. Joseph had booked rooms for them at a nearby hotel. Most of their time was spent at the hospital except to clean up and sleep a few hours.

Callie had notified the university and Heather that David had been in a serious accident and she didn't plan to return. She called Jesse's folks and his dorm and relayed the same message.

The fifth morning after the accident, as Callie was returning from the hotel, Joseph stopped her outside David's room. "Callie, David is very eager to speak with you this morning." They walked into his room and as soon as she touched his hand, his eyes opened and he managed a smile. She leaned down and kissed his cheek. In a weak but determined voice, he whispered, "Marry me."

Tears rushed to her eyes. "Other than you stabilizing and getting out of this hospital, there's nothing I want more, David. As soon as you are able, we will marry. You concentrate on getting better."

"Marry me ... today, Callie. Please!" He was pleading with his eyes as well as his voice and words, and she lost her composure.

Weeping, she moved close and kissed him gently. "I want to be your wife and I want you for my husband, but Honey, we can't do that, not here, not now. We don't have a marriage license or a preacher. The most important thing is you getting well enough to leave this place."

He nodded to his dad. Callie looked at Joseph who held up a marriage license.

"How?" she asked.

He motioned her outside the room. "From the time he re-gained consciousness yesterday and realized that he's not going to get out of this hospital alive unless we have a Lazarus miracle, he has been communicating his wish to marry you. Special exceptions have been made in this case and all you need is a minister. Pastor Walker is in the waiting area."

With tears still rolling down her cheeks, Callie went back into David's room. She looked at him … remembering New Year's Eve and the early hours of the New Year. She could not refuse him. "Yes, David, I'll marry you today. Can we wait for my folks?"

He nodded and his smile cheered her hurting heart. She called her parents. They left immediately.

While they were waiting, Joseph gave David and Callie time alone. He had picked up their wedding bands yesterday and brought the wedding vows that David had written the day after Christmas.

Words were hard for David, but he kept thanking her for loving him. "David, the last three weeks with you have been the best and happiest of my life, not to mention life changing. You've helped me understand that a love relationship with God is possible and desirable. She hugged and kissed him as much as the equipment would allow. Both wept. God's love was filling them … in spite of their circumstances.

Callie's parents and Carla arrived two hours later. Five days after their engagement, with the pastor, Joseph, her parents, Carla and some of the nurses looking on, David and Callie were getting married.

Pastor Walker, struggling with his own words, referenced Ecclesiastes 4:12 and spoke of the three strand cord in a marriage with God as the third thread. He reminded them that the physical joining is temporary but the union of their spirits with God is eternal.

When it came time for the vows, David requested that Callie read the ones he had written. She took the copy from Joseph's hand.

*Callie, I take you to be my wife, my constant friend, my faithful companion and my forever love, to have and hold, to honor and treasure from this day forward.* She paused to wipe the tears that were clouding her vision. *In the presence of God, our family and friends, I give all of me and all I have to you. I promise to keep myself for you alone.* She hesitated again to maintain control of her voice. David's vows were expressing God's unselfish love. *I give you my solemn vow to love you in sickness and in health, in good times and bad, in joy and in sorrow. I promise to love you unconditionally and sacrificially, to support you in your goals and respect you, to laugh with you and cry with you, and to cherish you above all others as long as we both shall live.*

Callie leaned down and kissed him. "I understand those vows much better today than I would have two weeks ago. I'd like to use them as my vows to you. Is that okay?" He smiled and nodded.

Though she had to pause several times, Callie made his vows hers to him. Both wept as the impact of covenant took effect. Rings were exchanged. Pastor Walker pronounced them man and wife. Callie helped David sign the marriage license.

David Henderson's dream of six plus years had become a reality. Callie was his bride. They kissed and as Callie pulled back, David's soft, sweet chuckle lightened sad hearts. He smiled as though he had no pain or problems. Everyone smiled ... and everyone cried.

Callie left his side only for necessities after that. Admittedly the hospital was not an ideal place to spend a honeymoon, but David and Callie didn't complain. They had each other and for now -- that was enough.

Folks gave them as much privacy as possible. They shared sweet memories and spoke of their future when he was awake. Much of the time words weren't even necessary. Callie found herself touching him, caressing him, loving him when he was awake and pleading for his life as he slept.

Marriage agreed with him. He had a more restful night and appeared stronger the next morning. Around noon, he motioned Callie to his side. She kissed his lips warmly and he smiled. With much effort, he moved his arm to her back and tried to pull her close. He asked her to get the nurse.

Thinking that he was in need of help, she turned on the call light. When one of the older nurses walked into the room, he motioned her closer. He pointed to all the medical support connected to him. "Take it off! All of it!" She tried to explain that she couldn't do that. Still he kept pointing and repeating, "Take-it-off!"

The nurse left and immediately called the doctor in charge. Within an hour, the doctor walked into the room. "I hear you want these tubes and machines removed, David. Is that your wish?"

David nodded.

The doctor looked at Callie and motioned her to step outside the room. "As his wife you now hold power of attorney over his care. He wants all medical support removed. I won't do that without your approval."

"Oh, I can't make that decision. Let's find his father."

She finally located Joseph in the chapel. He was crying. She slipped into the pew next to him and reached for his hand. As gently as she could, she conveyed David's request to remove all medical support.

He sat there a few more minutes then rose and pointed her to the door. They had the doctor notified.

Joseph asked the doctor if there was any possibility that his son could pull through this. The doctor shook his head as he explained that David's vital signs were beginning to indicate the end was near. He expressed belief that David knew that and wanted some time without the medical support that could no longer help him. He assured them that removing it would not affect the outcome, but it might offer David a more peaceful death. He promised they would keep him as comfortable as possible.

How do you sign such papers? What do you tell yourself? Callie's hand could not and would not pick up the pen. Joseph had already faced similar choices with Ella and with tears streaming down his cheeks, he signed the papers first.

Callie kept reminding herself that this was David's request. She picked up the pen and began to write. She managed the C-a-l-l-i-e but when she progressed to the last name, she dropped the pen. His last name was now hers. She couldn't do it. The doctor told her that his dad's signature was enough. She nodded her thanks.

Almost immediately staff began to remove tubes and machines. David expressed his gratitude when it was all cleared out. The atmosphere of the room changed. He looked better. He was still tall, dark and handsome ... and he was her husband. *My love for him consumes me, Lord. If it's true that You love him more, why this?*

*Trust me, Daughter. Trust me!*

David motioned to his dad and pointed at the door. Joseph seemed to know what his son had in mind. He leaned down and spoke of his love, kissed him and walked out. David then looked at Callie and she leaned close. "Lay with me," he softly entreated.

She looked at him and smiled. "There's no room for me, husband of mine. You take up most of this thing they call a bed."

He kept insisting, so Callie called the nurse in and explained David's request. The nurse smiled and called an orderly to help. They maneuvered David as gently as possible closer to the edge with the rails up on his side. Then they left.

He didn't have to ask her again. As carefully and gently as possible, Callie eased her body onto the narrow bed so that she and her beloved were resting face to face. David whispered, "I love you, Wife." And with a smile that was reminiscent of her sweet David, he asked weakly, "Ready for that smooching marathon?"

As tears cascaded down the side of her face, she leaned in and kissed him with as much passion as the moment permitted. "I love you, Husband. I'm not running away this time!' She embraced him to the extent that she could, spoke of her love while she caressed his battered and broken body. His love engulfed her. Their hearts beat as one.

"This love we are sharing overwhelms me, David. Do you think it's possible to be overwhelmed by God's love?"

Tears were freely rolling down David's cheeks now. "Yes, Callie, I do. And if I don't make it out of this hospital alive, promise me that you will trust His love for all your tomorrows." He was more emotional that she had ever seen him and as the tears continued rolling down his cheeks he added, "And someday, you might want to give that Oklahoma cowboy another chance."

All her control crumbled and her tears joined his. "Oh, please don't say things like that, David. I cannot imagine ever loving anyone like I love you. You are here and I'm treasuring every minute we have together."

Much of their time was spent simply cherishing the gift of each other and going together into God's secret place and soaking in His love. They poured out their hearts about their current situation and hopes for their future, but knew the final outcome was His. They loved and were loved ... by each other and their God.

January 9th, in the late afternoon, Callie noticed a change. She crawled in bed with him and held him close. This time he didn't respond. Still she spoke of her love and God's. A few hours later, she felt him struggle. She hugged him tighter hoping to hang on a little longer while begging God for a Lazarus moment. Then with a love that trumped every selfish yearning inside her, she whispered, "David, if it's best for you to go, I release you."

Suddenly peace flooded the room and her heart. David's body relaxed. Death had been swallowed up by LIFE. She knew the instant he left because part of her went with him. There was a holy stillness lingering in the room. Her heart felt empty and full all at the same time.

Not too long afterwards she eased herself away from his body ... and struggled to breathe without him in her life. With pain that threatened to remove all consciousness, she gently removed his wedding band. Unclasping the chain holding their double heart pendant, she threaded the chain through his ring and put the necklace on again. Taking a deep breath, she walked out of his room and Joseph knew. They embraced and shared the love and loss of a husband and a son.

## CHAPTER 36

Jesse had been out of his mind since receiving the second hand message from Callie. The first day of school he left a note for Heather to meet him in the lobby of her dorm after supper.

He was a bundle of nervous energy. "Heather, what do you know about Callie and David? If I didn't have school and football practice, I'd take a road trip and find out for myself what is going on."

"Nothing more than the first message which was disturbing for sure. I've called her home several times. A couple of times no one answered. The other times her mom has answered and simply said Callie was still at the hospital with David. She offers nothing more. If she's staying at the hospital with him, it must be pretty serious. And the fact that she mentioned not coming back to school could indicate a long recovery time ahead that Callie feels she has to be part of. What have you heard?"

"Nothing more than the original message. You'd think she would call one of us and give us an update. My thoughts and emotions are twisted up inside me, Heather. I'm sorry David has been hurt, but I don't understand why Callie would put her life on hold as a result. I keep wondering if anything was resolved between them before the accident. Surely she's not staying out of guilt. I cannot accept losing that girl. Would you mind calling again to see if there is an update?"

"I'll call tonight and let you know."

"Thanks."

Heather did call that night and every night after that until she got an answer. Callie's mom answered but still refused to give any details.

"Callie's life has drastically changed, Heather. She wants to be the one to explain. You'll hear from her within the next couple of weeks."

Heather relayed that message to Jesse. "Drastically changed? What in the name of all that is holy does that mean?" Jesse implored. "If I were a cursing or drinking man, I'd do both about now. Guess I'll go work out an extra hour or two instead. I'm not sure my body or mind can cope with two more weeks of not knowing."

## CHAPTER 37

Eight days after David put his ring back on her finger, the bride of three days was a twenty year old widow. His earthly assignment had been twenty-two years and seven months.

She knew all the things she was supposed to do and say; but knowing and doing are poles apart sometimes, and this was one of those times. *God, this does not feel like unselfish love. This feels cruel and unnecessary. You've taken the person who opened my heart to a personal relationship with You. Why?*

She had been gloriously happy and now she was profoundly empty. If not for Joseph and her parents, she would resign from life. They kept pointing her to the Author of life and reminding her that all life on earth is temporary. Yes, but twenty-two is too temporary. Why wasn't the sixty-eight year old drunk with a rap sheet as long as he was tall, killed instead? Why David?

When she felt herself sinking, she'd watch Joseph. How had he survived the last four years of his life? First he buried his wife. Now he would place the body of his only living child next to hers. David had told him about the baby. No grandchildren from his loins on this earth, but Heaven was rich with his family. Why was he not bitter? How was his faith still intact? Maybe his name was really Job.

Joseph handled the funeral arrangements. Callie was grateful. She had not been able to look at his vacant body yet. The memories of him alive were too fresh and vivid. She had some serious questions to ask God … when she got brave enough to hear the answers.

The days following his death were exhausting. She wasn't sure how she was surviving. Well-meaning folks stopped by the house. Asked questions about the marriage. Made comments. Offered advice.

Then came the family viewing. Callie had tried to prepare herself but she had failed. Seeing his body lying there without him in it was indescribable. What was left of her heart fractured into a thousand pieces.

Joseph recognized the pain and pulled her aside. He pulled a New Testament with the Psalms out of his coat pocket and shared a verse from Psalm thirty-four. "Listen to the words of this verse, Callie. *The Lord is near to the brokenhearted and saves the crushed in spirit.* God is near. He's here. He knows our hearts are broken. He sees our crushed spirits. He will not let go of us. We can't turn from Him in this. Instead, we must run to Him.

"He understands the pain of love and loss. He also knows that life comes out of death. That's where we have to trust. At first I was angry with Him for taking my wife and now my only son, but Callie, He gave His only Son for me … and Ella and David … and you, and just as He was reunited with His Son, so we will be with our David. We have lost him for a season, but because we are joined with him in Christ, we will be together again. This is not the end. That's our hope and our comfort."

"I'm not sure I could have accepted that from anyone else, Uncle Joseph," she conceded. "I know your pain and loss is greater than mine, and yet you believe."

That conversation took her back to the one she and David had. God loved her even more than David and she needed to find a private place and time to be with Him, because right now half of her was missing and she was angry with God.

She did notice one thing sweet and beautiful happening. Joseph was being pulled into her family. She loved her folks and Carla for that. David would have been pleased.

The hills and valleys emptied as folks flocked to the visitation and funeral. That's the way of southern folks. That and food. There were plenty of both. Her words were few as the folks expressed their love for

David and their sympathy for her and Joseph. Mostly she listened and let the tears have their way.

She was surprised when David's teammates showed up. Nestled among them was Josie. Even though Callie had worked through the problems Josie had caused she was not prepared to deal with her here ... not now. She wasn't sure she could. She immediately began to look for Joseph.

Bless Him. He had already spotted Josie and moved quickly to Callie's side. He became the buffer she needed to gracefully make it through the rest of their visit. Before they left, however, Josie stepped beside Callie and spoke, even though Joseph was in hearing range.

"Callie, I am genuinely sorry for your loss. I hope one day some man loves me as much as David loved you." Callie could not speak. Joseph stepped between them, thanked Josie for coming and walked her out the door behind the team.

Callie had to seek a quiet place. She refused to associate memories of Josie with her memories of David. What the enemy had meant for destruction, God had used for good. Out of the ashes of selfishness, God's unselfish love had risen. Callie could not let go of that kind of love. It suddenly became clear now that Josie's search for love in the physical realm was just a symptom of her lack of a love relationship with God. Now she knew how to pray for her.

Joseph sought her out after the team and Josie left. "Are you okay, Callie?"

"I will be, Uncle Joseph. Thanks for running interference."

"Callie, I don't think she meant to cause you any further pain. I believe she may be seeking for answers in her own life, but this was not the time nor the place for that to happen."

January 12, 1977, was a cold, sunny day in the hills of Virginia. They had made it through the funeral and burial and were leaving the grave site. Callie was not only weary and exhausted physically but also experiencing emotions that kept her vacillating between gratefulness and despair. Worse than that, she had no idea what the future held. In twelve days she had gone from a euphoric high with his ring back on her finger to a hospital wedding and honeymoon to watching them throw dirt on his casket. She was the now the proverbial ship without a rudder being tossed around by forces beyond her control.

Joseph pulled Callie aside and asked if he could visit with her and her parents tonight. They made plans for 7 o'clock. She looked at him and marveled at his strength. Yes, he wept and grieved but he wasn't falling apart. She felt so close to the edge at times.

Joseph arrived on time and the five of them spent some time sharing memories of David. They smiled and laughed, but mostly they grieved. There would always be secrets that only Callie and Joseph knew.

Finally Joseph looked at Callie. "I spent some time in David's room the day after he died and I found this." He handed her a black leather book. "If you look inside you will find that it was a book of blank pages, many now filled. I only read the first and last pages and realized it is the journal of his love for you. The first entry was the night of your sixteenth birthday. The last entry was New Year's Eve before he picked you up. It belongs to you."

Callie clutched that book to her heart as though a piece of David himself had been given back to her. Tears flowed freely. Words did not.

"I have decided to leave his room as it is until you are up to helping me go through his things. We'll know when it is time. Maybe summer."

Clearly, Joseph was making every effort to hold himself together. "Callie, David's love for you prompted the marriage, but it encompassed much more than those few days you shared as man and wife." He was visibly shaken. "Tonight I am following David's death bed instructions … and they come with my full approval.

"He was the only family I had left." He didn't try to stop the tears anymore. "By marrying you, David gave me a daughter. That was part of his plan. You've already found a place in my heart. I invite you to become part of my life with your parents' permission and blessing."

John and Beth wept and nodded approval. Callie's tears were non-stop by this point. Her head was congested. Tissues were littering the floor. Beth kept an arm around her as if trying to absorb some of her pain. Carla sat on the other side.

Joseph was more emotional than anyone had seen him since the accident. "I don't believe you were aware that David had substantial financial assets, Callie. His maternal grandparents left him a partial inheritance and gave the rest to Ella. When she died, all of it became his. He was a wise investor. You are a wealthy widow, Callie."

"Oh, Uncle Joseph, I didn't know he had any money. In all our times together, he never mentioned it. I don't want David's money. That's not why I married him."

He smiled through his tears. "We both realized that, Callie. David knew your love was unselfish, and that was your most precious gift to him and it made his toughest days on earth his happiest.

"One of the biggest reasons he insisted on marrying you before he died was to provide for your future."

Before they could wrap their minds around that life changing revelation, Joseph released another newsflash.

"There is more, and remember that I'm honoring his decisions. When he graduated, I turned over forty percent of the business assets to him. Those will be transferred to you. And Callie, one day everything I own will be yours. Ella and I had already told David that the house would be his the day he married. That was going to be his wedding gift to you. He wanted to fill it with children."

And with the thoughts and losses those words generated, Joseph unashamedly wept for the children David and Callie would never have and the grandchildren he would never hold.

The revelation of David's extravagant provision and sharing the pain of no offspring of David with Joseph, released waves of gratitude mixed with surges of sorrow that moved Callie to her knees in front of the man who had lost so much. Her dad and mom knelt beside her and jointly they all mourned their loss, yet gave thanks for the years of knowing David Henderson. No one rushed. Grieving together was binding them together.

Later, John and Joseph talked privately while the ladies prepared coffee and hot chocolate.

After the hot drinks were served, John opened a new conversation. "Callie, have you given any thought to what you are going to do now?"

Callie shook her head. "I have no idea, Dad. We planned to get married last week and I was going to transfer to our local college. Now my mind draws a blank when I try to think of the future without David."

"As difficult as it might be, Joseph and I suggest you considering going back to OU and finishing up this year." Looking at Beth, he continued. "All of us will support you whether you decide to go or stay home. With David gone and all your memories of him here, a change of scenery for a few months and plenty to occupy your mind might be more beneficial at this time."

Joseph added, "If you choose to go, we will take care of the financial end of David's business when you come home this summer or we can fly you home if it needs to be done sooner. The lawyers should have all the papers in order and maybe we will both be ready to deal with his personal belongings by then."

Beth looked at Callie. "I haven't mentioned it, but Heather has called several times seeking information about David's accident and your uncertain return to school. I only affirmed what you had shared. I never mentioned the marriage, his death or your plans. You are the one to share that information when you are ready."

"Thanks, Mom."

"Callie, there is one more thing I forgot to mention," Joseph added. "Ella had some family keepsakes that I want to give to you. Some heirloom quilts, family jewelry, her last doll and a few other items. I put them in one of her old family trunks. Let me know when you are ready for them."

"She showed me some of those things one day, Uncle Joseph. I'll treasure them."

Tears were gathering in Joseph's eyes again. "As David's father, I thank you for loving and marrying my son, Callie. He wasn't the only one who loved unselfishly. Thank you for accepting his ring ... both times. He was a rare young man and I'm proud to have been his dad. The last time we were together, we prayed that the Lord would work things out with Jesse if he didn't make it. That was a difficult prayer for him to pray, Callie. He wanted to grow old with you. Some things just aren't meant to be."

Callie didn't try to hide her tears from him or her family. "Uncle Joseph, how am I supposed to deal with this? I know you understand. I feel so lost without him. All my hopes and dreams for the future were buried with him today. And sometimes I feel like this love we shared is going to smother me, it is so tangible. Does the pain ever go away? Will the love always be with me?"

Now Joseph was weeping again. "The love never dies, Callie. The pain of the loss does lessen with time, but there will always be moments when the loss of what could have been will surface. Take it one day at a time. Call me. We'll grieve together. As for your future, in time you will find that God has simply changed your directions. He will bring you through this."

Over the next few days she and her parents discussed and prayed about her immediate plans. After carefully weighing the pros and cons and listening to the still small voice she was beginning to recognize, she decided to check with OU and see if it was too late to return. After hearing of her situation, they agreed to work with her. A flight was booked and Heather was alerted for pickup on January 19th.

## Chapter 38

On the trip to OU, Callie recalled her flight home in December and replayed the life changing events that had taken place since. It felt like a time warp. When she questioned the reality of it all, one look at the bracelet and rings silenced all doubts. David was gone. She was praying that the unexpected meltdowns triggered by the inevitable ebb and flow of memories or the reality of life without him wouldn't happen in public settings.

As the plane neared the landing strip, she was reminded that much more than her name had changed. She had changed.

When she saw Heather, images of sweet, persistent Jesse dropping her off almost six weeks ago surfaced and the reality of facing him hit head on. He was going to be crushed. Maybe she should take the next flight back home. As she and Heather shared greetings, Heather grabbed her left hand. "For crying out loud, Callie! Did you marry David?" Callie managed a nod and tears began to cascade down her cheeks.

Heather looped her arm through Callie's and began to walk her towards the baggage claims area. "Thunderation, Girl! No wonder you didn't call!"

Callie couldn't stop the tears. So much for control. Heather stopped abruptly. "Wait a minute! What are you doing in Oklahoma?" Passengers were having to walk around them, but Heather was desperate for answers. "Girlfriend, I cannot believe this!" She grabbed Callie's hand and pulled her to the side. "I'm sorry if I'm adding to your stress, but this is not logical. Why are you here? And where is David?"

Wanting to get away from the crowd, Callie managed, "Heather, it is a ... complicated story. Let's get to the car ... and I'll tell you."

As Heather drove, Callie, with many tears and much pain, highlighted her holiday break. She shared everything except the money. Heather was dumbfounded.

"Merciful Heaven, I didn't know that much could happen to someone in six weeks. I think complicated is an understatement."

Both were quiet for a few minutes. "Jumping Jehoshaphat, Callie! What about Jesse? I don't know whom I feel sorrier for ... you ... or him."

"It's not going to be easy ... for either of us. Please don't let him know I'm here yet. I still don't know how to tell him any of this."

"Uh-oh! Callie, I've already alerted him that I was picking you up. He's excited that you've come back but scared about what happened between you and David over the holidays. He questioned why you didn't ask him to meet you. Now I know. Boy, oh boy."

Callie let the conversation die at that point. She was weary and still had much to accomplish today.

After getting settled in the dorm, submitting her name change information to the Records Office and picking up her class assignments for the semester, Callie headed to her classes and the library for the day. She changed her study spot so curious Jesse could not find her ... not today. She wasn't ready for that emotional encounter.

Busy with a purpose felt good. If facing Jesse wasn't looming over her like a bad forecast, she could see the benefits of getting back in school. After a couple of hours of studying, she laid her head down to rest for a few minutes.

While Callie was resting, Jesse was searching ... for her ... in Bizzell. Silly girl. Since when did a new study spot stop him? His heart went into overdrive when he saw her. His list queen was back. How was David? What had transpired between them? He wanted to hug her, but then he wanted to lecture her for not calling. He pulled out a chair opposite her hoping the pleasure of being close would keep his uneasiness at bay. It didn't work. He had too many questions that needed answers. His fidgeting roused Callie.

As she opened her eyes, she was greeted by God's hand sculptured male model and a monsoon of guilt joined her overtaxed emotions. Drowning seemed imminent. Callie put her head in her hands in surrender. That's when Jesse spotted the rings. Callie raised her head to find his body frozen but his facial expressions were revealing the impact the moment was having on his heart and mind. He stared between her rings and her face. His chair fell backwards as he sprang up and shoved it out of the way.

He was speechless too long to suit Callie. "If you'll sit down, Jesse, I'll try to explain." A stormy expression began to cloud his face and she knew that sitting was not going to happen. Rather, she sensed a rather large tsunami approaching the west wing of Bizzell.

"Oh, I don't think you need to explain anything, Callie. Those rings tell me more than I want to know. No wonder you didn't bother to call." The mime had come to life and now he was pacing and ranting like a madman. "You married the man! He not only convinced you to put the engagement ring back on, he finally got a wedding band on that finger. Well, guess what. I don't want to hear your explanations, Mrs. Henderson!"

At this point, Jesse was neither quiet nor discreet. "Callie, this is asinine. Where is David anyway? And what about his accident. It didn't keep you from getting married, did it?"

"Jesse, please sit down … and listen." Callie didn't even try to stop the tears. She was trying to survive.

"Listen to what? How he wooed you? How he made you forget I existed? No, thanks, Callie."

He was furious … and rightly so. If he would just listen, but before she could get another word out, another wave hit. "None of this makes any sense, Callie. I think you both belong in the looney bin."

Callie knew she and Jesse were reaping the pain of her selfish choices. Finally she managed to speak between sobs of pain that matched his fury. "It's … complicated … Jesse."

"Oh, is that what you call it?" He shouted louder with a mocking voice while intently eyeing her for the next attack.

"I think insane describes it better. Obviously Lover Boy didn't fly back with you. Trouble in Paradise already, Callie? What kind of husband allows his new bride to fly a thousand miles away so she can go back to school … without him? The wreck must have addled his brain. You can bet your bottom dollar that this Oklahoma boy would have kept you home."

Her body was trembling as her mind and emotions were fighting to survive that last wave. His wrath and her guilt were smothering her. *God, why didn't you take my life instead of David's? I'm the one causing all the pain. I'm the one screwing everything up. My selfishness probably killed David and now it is crushing Jesse. Just. Let. Me. Die.*

Not moved by her delicate physical or emotional state, Jesse set the final wave in motion. "I'm out of here. Callie Henderson, I hope I never see you again in my life, but if I do, I'll turn in the opposite direction." And he walked away.

She could not be strong any longer. Her mind short circuited. Her emotions were shutting down. Her body was racked with exhaustion. She finally passed out or fell asleep.

She had no idea how long she had been there after Jesse left before she felt a gentle touch on her shoulder. She looked up and there stood Kirk, Jesse's roomie. "Are you okay, Callie?"

"No." His gentle touch and presence brought her back from the brink as feelings and thoughts re-emerged. He pulled a chair beside her and gently pulled her into a caring embrace. He didn't say a word. He just held her. When she began to regain some composure, he softly commented. "Jesse is devastated, Callie. You don't seem to be doing any better. What is going on?"

She took a deep breath as his calm, caring disposition supplied the fortification she had needed. "Would you walk me to my dorm, Kirk? I have a story to tell you." He carried her books in one arm and offered her the other. They walked slowly. He listened. She cried and for the second time since losing David, she shared their story. Again she saw no reason to mention the money.

"Does Jesse know?"

"Are you kidding? He saw the rings and the thought of me married to David angered him beyond listening to any explanation. He hasn't been quiet long enough to hear anything I have to say. And you, my friend, are not allowed to tell him. This must come from me.

"Kirk, I'm dealing with guilt and regret over David as well as loss and grief. My involvement with Jesse compounds the guilt. But I can't go back. I can only deal with today. I have to tell him. He won't like it, but he must hear it. I'll find a way."

She paused and looked into the eyes of Jesse's gentle, caring roommate, "Thanks for listening, Kirk. Thanks for being concerned for both of us."

"I don't know what to say, Callie. I can't imagine your loss of David nor the conflict you must be experiencing with Jesse. He's a total mess. I hope you find a way to tell him soon." He put his arm around her shoulders and pulled her in for a big brother hug. She didn't know how much she needed human touch until now. She leaned into him as they walked. Calmness slowly began to claim her body, mind and emotions. "Thanks, Kirk."

"I'm a phone call away, Callie. Anytime."

Kirk was genuine and a gentleman. "Thanks again." And she walked into the dorm.

Callie turned to the only One who could help. *God, I need help with Jesse.* Before she could finish the prayer, she knew she had to go see his folks.

She finished her classes for the week and even though she needed to spend the weekend catching up, she called Kirk and asked to borrow his truck. She explained her plan to visit Jesse's folks. He delivered the truck mid-afternoon Friday and she headed to the Collins ranch.

## Chapter 39

As Callie pulled in the driveway, Margaret stepped out of the house and Dean approached from the barn. "I'm sorry to barge in like this, but I desperately need to talk with Jesse and right now he's not interested in listening."

They were kind, but guarded. "He called to tell us you are married. Callie, Jesse is shattered! I've never seen my boy in such a state. His anger is just covering his deep hurt and loss. Surely you understand that." Dean was rightfully defending his son while checking out an antique set of rings.

"I do, Mr. Collins. But there's more to the story. If you'll hear me out, I'll do whatever you suggest after that."

"Fair enough," Margaret said as she led the way to the house.

They offered Callie a drink and then settled around the dining room table. Calmly and as detailed as the situation warranted, she shared the events of her holiday break, starting with the accident. She purposely avoided mentioning that she and David were engaged before the accident. Margaret's tears soon joined Callie's as she told of David's death. She ended with her decision to return to school and her encounter with Jesse. She made no mention of the money.

"There's only one thing to do," Dean said. "We have to get our boy home. Now!"

Dean informed Jesse's dorm supervisor that a family crisis had arisen and requested Jesse be alerted as quickly as possible. It was the weekend; he wouldn't miss any classes.

In the meanwhile, Callie, waiting for the storm to arrive, was fed and collapsed in Lizzie's room. Regardless of how Jesse's folks felt about the marriage, they were genuinely sorry about David's death. That brought a measure of comfort. Facing the fury of Jesse? That was a different story.

Within minutes she was asleep. A couple of hours later the sound of an approaching vehicle caused her to stir. Dean had decided to hide Kirk's truck, so Jesse had no idea she was inside the house. Dean and Margaret were calmly waiting for him at the big dining room table.

Jesse entered with the energy of an approaching storm. "Okay, give. What is going on around here? I've tried to figure out what could be wrong and all sorts of things have run through my mind? So out with it." He couldn't sit, so he paced and pushed his fingers through his longer, curly blonde hair.

"First, why don't you sit down and tell us what is going on between you and Callie," his dad suggested.

"Earth to Dad! She married David over the holidays! A husband is between us! I tried to tell you." Nervous energy was radiating off him like a family of hovering hummingbirds.

"Yeah, but you were so upset that we wondered if you got all the facts," Margaret commented.

"Look, Mom. When there's a wedding band on her finger and she admits that she married him, what else is there to know? Do you think this is some kind of cruel joke? If so, I don't appreciate her sense of humor."

"Did you give her a chance to explain what happened and why?" Margaret asked.

"No disrespect intended, Mom, but you don't get it. *The what* is obvious and I don't think my heart can handle *the why*. So no, I didn't stick around long enough for her to explain."

"Well, Son, I can tell you first hand that there is much more to her story and you owe it to yourself and her to listen," Dean added.

That statement stopped Jesse in his tracks. With a cold stare that questioned his dad's sanity he asked, "And how would you know that, Dad?"

"Because they took the time to listen," replied a soft voice from the hall.

Jesse glared at them and then turned to face Callie with anger and pain so raw that she crumbled inside and outside. Seeing again the pain she had inflicted on him brought her to her knees. *You took the wrong person, God. Why didn't you take me?* She cried as she buried her face in her hands. If the Lord didn't take her, maybe she would just become a nun.

Dean moved to Callie and led her to a chair at the table. He turned to Jesse. "She is the family crisis, Son. Sit down, shut your mouth and open your mind and heart. For your sake and hers, you need to listen."

Jessie was speechless but obeyed his dad.

"I want the rest of the family to hear so you don't have to keep repeating this, Callie." Dean walked outside and rang the dinner bell. Five siblings entered the house.

"Sit down and listen, children. You need to hear the rest of the story." Lizzie moved close to Callie. Roger sat by Jesse and kept a wary eye on Callie.

She began her story with the accident … and tears. She fought for control of her voice and emotions. Reliving those times and events twice in one day was taking a toll on her. She purposely avoided mentioning the engagement or the money … again. This was not the time nor the place to share much more than bare facts. As the story began to unravel, so did Jesse's anger. Compassion and shame took turns roaming over his readable face as more of his anger and pain retreated. He seemed uneasy with the marriage, but when she got to David's death and the funeral, he was on his knees in front of her … silently sharing her grief and apologizing for adding to her pain.

Everyone sat quietly for a few minutes after she finished and then one by one walked away until only Jesse, Roger and Callie remained. Looking into her fatigued eyes, Jesse asked, "Can you forgive me, Callie?"

She nodded. Roger looked at Jesse. "Are you going to be okay, Bro?" Jesse nodded and Roger left them alone.

"Callie, I can't imagine what you have been through, and then you had to deal with all my madness. What can I say? I reacted badly. I am deeply sorry."

"And I'm sorry for the pain I've caused you, Jesse."

He moved to sit beside her. "I won't make excuses except to say that my heart took a nose dive when I saw those rings and my mind refused any explanation. I've never experienced emotions like that. That was an emotional Hiroshima. My world was blown apart, you were gone and I was lost. I'm glad you came back to school."

"My family and Uncle Joseph felt I'd do better coming back to school and staying busy rather than staying at home where memories of David are inescapable."

She was still crying. "I'm not only dealing with losing David, I'm dealing with the haunting question … could I have prevented his death if I had married him earlier? I wonder if my involvement with you cost David his life. Those thoughts torment me, Jesse. I have much to work through. There's more to the story but I'm not ready to share that right now. You and I can only be friends. And I don't know if that will ever change. I'll understand if you walk out of my life. I've been nothing but trouble and heartache to you."

David had always been between them … engaged or not, but Jesse sensed Callie's attachment to him in death was stronger than when he was alive. *Is that her guilt regarding his death?*

Trouble and heartache? Yeah, she had caused plenty of that since they met. Should he walk away? Could he walk away? Maybe he should, but he couldn't. No, not when there was a chance things could work out. There was hope. He was a patient man and this was his list queen. He could wait. "Callie, I'm not going anywhere. We've been friends before. We can be friends again."

Jesse pulled her to her feet and hugged her. Her response was subdued. She was serving him notice that things had changed. David was gone but it was apparent those expensive rings on her finger had cut Jesse off from her … again. He wasn't sure what their friendship was going to look like. Would loving this woman always be like this?

As he released her, he thanked her for caring enough to make him hear the truth. They walked outside and found his folks on the porch. She thanked them for helping and apologized for hurting Jesse. When she headed to the back of the barn, he followed her. The minute he spotted Kirk's truck he stopped her. "Why are you driving Kirk's truck?"

"How did you think I got here, Jess? I have no wheels. Kirk let me borrow his."

"Kirk knows about this?"

"Yeah, he rescued me after our initial meeting in the library and I shared with him. He was concerned for both of us. Don't be upset with him."

"Who else did you tell before me?"

"I told Heather the day I got back. I tried to tell you in the library, but you wouldn't listen. No one else knows."

She studied Jesse. "You need to get your list out again and give some other girls a chance. More than my last name has changed."

She had started reading David's journal and knew she would not be ready to deal with Jesse anytime soon. Reading the journal was like secret visits with David and she wasn't going to give that up for anyone."

"I'm not blind or dead, Callie. I see what's out there. I've set a high bar and so far you have no competition. I will probably date others, but I'll also be keeping an eye on you. Can't help it. It is what it is."

Callie drove away. Jesse stayed home.

Jesse didn't see Callie often that entire semester, but he kept tabs on her through Heather. It felt like their relationship had been downgraded to an acquaintance. Callie buried herself in school and left everyone else alone, except Heather. She had changed.

He tried dating other girls, but all he did was compare them to Callie and his list. That was no more help for his aching heart than school had been for Callie's. He was hopeful that home and summer would force her to deal with David's part in her life and bring them closer to a time of starting over. He wanted to plan a future with this woman and he had decided to hang around until that was possible.

When his folks or Roger questioned him about Callie, he told them she needed time and he was waiting.

The term ended and Heather drove Callie to the airport. Jesse headed for the ranch. They would spend the summer miles and states apart.

# Chapter 40

Callie had decided to accept Joseph's offer to work at the dealership. This was not a direction she would have chosen, but since it had been dropped in her lap, she wanted to check it out. She wanted to honor David.

To her surprise, healing was beginning to take place daily by simply spending time with her family and Joseph who understood her loss. That plus the business provided the therapy she needed. They grieved and laughed together. They celebrated David's life and mourned his death and their loss. They still marveled at the level of his unselfish thoughts and actions during his last days.

The lawyers and accountants tied up the business end of David's affairs, and when Callie Henderson found out the extent of David's resources, she was bowled over. This was a side of him she knew nothing about. She learned he had been a generous benefactor as well as a smart investor. Determined to follow his lead, she asked Joseph to be her financial advisor until she learned enough to be on her own. She felt the need to check out some possible business classes.

About four weeks into the summer, Joseph asked Callie if she was ready to help him with David's room. She felt she was. They made plans.

She hadn't been to the Henderson place since David's death. Turning onto the lane and approaching the house released a landslide of memories ... and tears. It was a great day for a horseback ride or throwing a hook in the water. It was warm enough for an afternoon at the old swimming hole, but David wasn't rushing to meet her with a smile that rivaled the sunrise. Her David was gone ... and he wasn't coming home again. The ache was familiar and loneliness had become her companion.

Joseph was sitting in a swing on the massive front porch. Seeing her tears and understanding her pain, he suggested she go in alone. "Take your time, Callie."

Walking into the house filled with memories of their past touched new places of loss. But it was the unfulfilled dreams of what could have been that hurt the most at this moment. This is where they would have lived and laughed and loved ... and raised their family.

Callie hesitated as she approached his room. She had never crossed the threshold. That had been one of their boundaries. As she stepped inside, the years of knowing him greeted her. She welcomed them. Closing her eyes, she could almost picture him. Down the hall. At the stables. Almost. Until his last time here registered. He had left this room to pick her up New Year's Eve and never returned.

Memories of that night still warmed her. She yearned to hear his voice. Longed to see his face. Ached for his touch. Seven months of days and nights without him all came together in this one space. And here for the first time since his death, she felt free to fully experience the pain of losing him. And she did. Alone in his room with the God who loves her more than even David, Callie got real.

She didn't pretend or try to be strong. She was honest and transparent. She poured it all out. Her guilt. Her regrets. Her anger. Her questions ... especially about the injustice of taking a young man who loved God and leaving an older man who cared more for his bottle than the life of another human being. Her love. Most of all her love. She laid on his bed and wept for the nights they would never have together and the children that would never be. In the place where new life could have been conceived, she released David back to the Giver of life. She felt God's presence here. Intimacy with David was no longer possible, but intimacy with God was. And He could handle her junk. He loved her and promised to never leave her.

One item in the room hit her hard. On the night stand by his bed was their engagement photo. Engraved on the pewter frame was the date, July 16, 1976. She held it close and wept. For a moment *the ifs* knocked. *If* they had married on that date, he would probably still be alive. *If* they had married on that day, she could well be carrying his child. *If* they had married that day ... She had learned to shut down *the ifs* of life. They paralyze, steal, kill and destroy, because they are opposite of faith. So she made the choice to treasure the photo and the memories but refuse the guilt that tried to attack.

His closet stirred her. The hint of his cologne unleashed another flood of memories long forgotten as she touched and hugged sweaters and shirts that had once been filled with him. Without him, they held no value, offered no appeal. They were reminders of all she once had and all she had lost. David's handsome outer man had attracted her, but his inner man wooed and won her. He was a man with a gentle heart and loving spirit. Even after his sin, it was his repentant heart and unrelenting love that drew her back.

Time was passing and yet so many things invited her attention. Knowing Joseph wouldn't mind, she lingered. Remembering. Treasuring. Releasing. There were moments she sensed David's presence so strongly she was certain that if she could pull back the veil between time and eternity that she would see him. And that thought turned her full attention to her forever love. The One who created her for His love. *I am my Beloved's, and He is mine.* Even death would not separate her from Him.

Before calling Joseph, she thanked God for the gift that David had been and still was. Because of him she had experienced some of life's greatest joys and deepest sorrows. And she was finding that life's greatest pains had produced some of God's greatest lessons and revealed some of His deepest truths.

Better prepared for the task before them, she called Joseph and together they packed his clothing and personal items that could be given to other folks. Each held back their choice treasures. Memories were shared and tears were shed.

When the task was completed, they knelt on different sides of his bed and thanked God for twenty-two years and seven months with

David Henderson. Much healing and closure took place that day for both of them.

Joseph dropped off Ella's trunk as Callie had requested and that night in the privacy of her room, Callie added her never worn wedding dress and veil, their marriage license, and the selected treasures from David's room to Ella's trunk of keepsakes. One day she'd add the engagement photo and his journal. Reading the journal was still therapeutic for her. He was teaching her how to be transparent and honest with herself and God, because he not only shared his successes but was bluntly honest about his failures. His heart was always beautiful even when his behavior was not.

As the hot, humid days of a Virginia summer were being marked off the calendar, Joseph noted Callie's knack and love for the business. With David gone, there was no family to carry on and she already owned forty percent of the stock, so he made her an offer. "Callie, would you be interested in becoming part of the day to day business operation of Henderson Enterprises when you graduate?"

"Oh, yes! Working with you this summer has opened my eyes to an unexpected career possibility. I've been thinking about picking up a couple of business classes my last two semesters."

"Then let's plan on it. You can pick up any additional courses you might need from one of the local colleges or even attend UV a summer or two after you graduate."

"Thank you, Uncle Joseph."

That conversation gave new direction to the rest of the summer and her life. She wasn't drifting anymore. Her future had a rudder again and with that came a direction.

A couple of weeks before she had to return to OU, Joseph called her into his office. "Callie, I've enjoyed working with you this summer, but even more than that, I've enjoyed spending time with my new daughter. That has eased my loss of David. And speaking of David … don't you think it's time to remove those rings? You are a widow, not a wife."

He looked at his ringless left hand as liquid pooled behind his lids. "I know it's a tough decision. Their love will forever be part of us.

Removing the rings signifies a willingness to accept life without them. Are you there, yet?"

"I'm close. How can you accept a wife dying of cancer and a son being killed by a drunk and not be angry at God? I've watched you and I don't see any traces of anger. You now have a wife and four children in heaven."

"Remember the verse from Matthew 6:21? *For where your treasure is, there will your heart be also.*" The things that matter the most in this life are already in heaven, Callie. Piece by piece, my heart has followed them. I think David took any part that was left."

The tears that had been pooling behind his eyelids began to drop one by one. "Callie, in a perfect world, my family would still be with me, but we live in a fallen world. That's not God's fault. He created a perfect one and we just keep messing it up. When bad things happen to good people in our messed up world, I choose to trust that God's love will triumph. I know my family is with the Lord, which according to Paul is far better, so how can I be angry?

"It is we who grieve, not them. Don't let the pain and loss of the past close you off to God's plans for your future. Your time and life with David on earth have come to an end. That wasn't your choice or doing. That was God's.

"You will always love David and his love will always be with you, but God has made our hearts big enough to love again. It will be a different love and it will not diminish or replace the love you shared with David.

"You are twenty-one and life awaits you. Embrace it. Keep in mind that David knew about Jesse's love for you, Callie. It gave him comfort when he realized he wouldn't be here for you. Don't be afraid to love again."

"There is a fear in me about loving again, Uncle Joseph. Loving again means to risk losing again and I don't think my heart could survive losing someone else. Which leads me to ask you a question. What about you? Aunt Ella's been gone over four years."

Realizing he had set himself up for that question, he chuckled. "Oh Callie, I'm not closed to finding love again. If or when God brings a lady into my life that stirs this heart of mine, I'll definitely check out the possibilities. So far I've simply not been attracted to any available ladies and I'm content with that. And besides, she'll have to pass your approval before I consider getting too serious, so you'll be one of the first to know."

"I've seen a couple of the single ladies in church glance your way more than once, Joseph Henderson. Does this mean you haven't noticed or there's no interest?"

"A man would have to be blind to not notice, Callie. There's no interest on my part. If you find one you are super impressed with, let me know. I trust your judgment. In the meanwhile, I enjoy life."

His secretary knocked at the entrance of the open door and alerted him of an appointment in five minutes.

"Give me four minutes and send him in."

He walked Callie to the door. "We'll talk more about the business when you graduate and have a better idea of your plans next summer." He laughed when he spotted her newly arrived, red Chevy Blazer. "Most college girls would have chosen a chic rather than a sporty vehicle, Callie."

"I was tempted to order a Corvette; but after David's accident, I couldn't. I decided the Blazer was more versatile."

Joseph and her dad had encouraged her to buy a new vehicle since she was planning to drive to Norman this fall. Having the means to buy things was still new to Callie. She continued to live by the frugal principles handed down by her parents. Not much had changed in her life, except she was always looking for opportunities to share. And like David, she opted to keep the knowledge of her wealth private.

She spent the next three days thinking and praying about removing her rings. On the eighth month anniversary of David's death, she tearfully made that choice. It wasn't easy.

Only his ring and the heart pendant necklace remained. Giving them up was tougher. One more night. She couldn't release their engagement photo yet either. One more night to hold them close. Tomorrow she would add them to her collection of treasures.

# Chapter 41

Out on the Great Plains, it wasn't the hot, dry summer that was troubling the Collins family. It was their eldest son. Jesse had been offered a night shift summer job working with the local law enforcement as an apprentice to a seasoned detective. His major advisor had worked it out so he could earn credit toward his degree.

Jesse knew his family was concerned about him. Though his brothers hassled him and his parents questioned him, he shared nothing.

He had multiple issues going on. His summer job had introduced him to a world foreign to him. He and Detective Richards had been assigned to a suspected drug ring investigation. About half way through the summer, evidence pointed to a suspected prostitution operation as well. He admired men and women who were wired to deal with such vices and the people involved. He now knew that he was not one of them. His experience had been educational in ways that the college credit would never reflect.

Shaking the images of the destitute people and his frustration over their twisted reasoning every morning after work was not easy. He tried to practice the Biblical direction of thinking on good things, hoping that by the time his body hit the sack, his mind would be at rest. Even if he did occasionally manage to accomplish that, trying to sleep with his noisy family in and out all day was about as likely as sleeping through a buffalo stampede. Crashing on his two days off was getting him through the ordeal.

Throw in his frustrating social life compared to Romeo Roger's newest flame and you had the perfect ingredients for a bummer summer.

The first of September, Margaret and Dean approached him with a suggestion. "Why don't you invite Callie to come spend a few days with us before school starts?"

"I don't know if that is a good idea," he countered. His confidence had taken a pounding when Callie married David and her reclusiveness last semester did nothing to repair the damage. He was hanging by a thin thread of hope to some of the statements she had made when he confronted her with his feelings last fall. He was so ready to move on. Was she?

Margaret smiled. "You'll never know if you don't ask." She stepped close and placed a caring hand on his arm. "She's young, Jesse. Her heart will heal, and she will love again. Maybe it's time to let her know that you are still interested. You are, aren't you?"

"You know I am, Mom."

He called that night. After talking around the world, he casually mentioned that his folks suggested she come for a visit before school started. To his surprise and delight, she liked the idea and agreed to head out the next day, if Shelby, a dorm friend, who lived in Nashville and was riding with her could be ready.

She was driving? She said something about needing a vehicle to get four years of accumulated belongings back home come spring. *Who cares? She's open to a visit!* Jesse felt like someone had opened the corral gate again. Happy days! Happy feet!

Shelby agreed. Callie alerted Jesse, packed and headed out early the next morning. She arrived in Nashville by evening and spent the night with Shelby. They left early the next morning and made it to OU late that night. Callie called to alert Jesse she had arrived and would see him tomorrow.

"I'll come pick you up tonight," he insisted. He was as restless as a squirrel locked in a cage all summer. Her willingness to come indicated her readiness for their relationship to move forward and he didn't intend to wait any longer than necessary.

"No, I haven't unpacked yet, I'll just drive on out. See you soon." She hung up before he could challenge her decision.

His thin thread of hope had given him the courage to put an engagement ring on layaway. Making those payments had been the only bright spot in his entire summer. God willing, one day it would be on her finger.

Reality wasted no time raining on that daydream. What did he have to offer her? His summer job had ruptured his dream of working in the criminal justice field to the point that he had been tempted to quit school. If not for Callie, he probably would have.

Now he would have to change majors which would entail a year or more of extra studies. Not graduating next spring meant no decent job. No decent job meant no wife. Callie would go back home. He was disgusted with himself.

A vehicle pulling into the driveway buried those depressing thoughts beneath the reality of seeing Callie. He was out the door before she could shut off the engine. He jerked her door open and without thinking reached in to hug her.

"Hey, Cowboy! I'm glad to see you, too. If you'll let me out, I think we can continue this warm welcome."

With that he reached one arm under her arms, another under her legs and lifted her out of the Blazer. "How's that for service, Ma'am?"

"Unusual and a little personal, but acceptable since it's you." She laughed, then laid her head on his shoulder and whispered, "I'm so tired, Jess."

He started carrying her towards the house. "Hey, I'm going to need my bag and purse."

No way was he putting her down. She was back in his arms and he intended to enjoy it for a few more minutes. She repeated, "Hey, you! I need my bag and purse."

"Not a problem. I'll come back and get them." He carried her into the house and placed her on a sofa in the den that was already made up for sleeping. "Since it's late, Mom thought it would be best not to wake Lizzie. Is that okay?"

"I could sleep anywhere right now." She snuggled up with the pillows provided as Jesse covered her with a light blanket and before he could kiss her on the cheek, she was asleep. He kissed her anyway.

He did his own version of the funky chicken dance back out to her vehicle. *Nice wheels for a college student. It has a cowgirl look to it. Wonder how she's paying for it. I guess Joseph must have gotten her a super deal. Maybe it was David's.*

He took her bag and purse and lightly set them on the floor by the sofa, turned off the lights and went to bed. Sleep didn't come. He had forgotten to check out her ring finger. He quietly slipped down the hall toward the den. He couldn't see her left hand; it was curled up under her head. He could wait a few more hours. He doubted he would sleep, so he stretched out in the lounge chair in the far corner of the room and waited for Callie to stir.

Several hours later he felt a light tap on his arm. When he opened his eyes, Lizzie was leaning over him. "Where is Callie, Jesse?"

He jerked the chair upright and peeked around Lizzie to see that the sofa was indeed empty.

"I don't know Lizzie. Have you tried the bathroom? Maybe she went to take a shower or -- you know -- rest."

Lizzie took off down the hall calling Callie's name. He heard her knock on the hall bathroom door. Callie responded. She must be cleaning up.

That was his clue. He needed to do the same.

Margaret and Dean were in the kitchen eating as the rest of the house began to stir. As they were finishing their breakfast, Callie walked in. They shared hugs and Margaret helped Callie get some food together.

While Callie was eating her breakfast, Jesse sauntered in and sat down beside her. His eyes were studying her hands. When she realized what he was doing, she placed her left hand on his and squeezed. He didn't care if his parents were in the kitchen taking it all in. He lifted her hand to his mouth and gently kissed that naked ring finger. He couldn't wait to put his ring there. "When?" he asked.

She pondered if this was the time and place to answer that question. She decided it was not the place but could be the time, so she nodded toward the door.

As they stepped out into the autumn air she responded, "Very recently, Jesse. Being home and working with David's dad this summer proved to be a season of healing for all of us. Uncle Joseph convinced me it was time to take the rings off and open my heart to a future with you ... if you are still interested."

Jesse stilled and stared ... and then wrapped her in a warm embrace. "If I'm still interested? Callie, there hasn't been a day since I met you that I've not been interested." He lifted her chin. "I love you, Mountain Woman."

And Jesse kissed Callie with two years of longing packed in one tender kiss. Tears began trickling down her cheeks.

"I know you've been through much, Cal. If I move too fast, will you tell me?" She nodded, laid her head on his shoulder and cried. He held her close and loved her quietly.

"Thanks, Jesse. Learning to turn loose of the past and embrace today is easier said than done. I will always love David, but Uncle Joseph told me that hearts can love again. I want to love again, Jesse, and I want it to be you. It's going to take some time."

Jesse looked into those chocolate doe eyes that had hypnotized him that first day in biology. "Well, that's okay because it seems it's going to be awhile before I can offer you anything but my love." He softly and gently kissed his girl again. Then he grabbed her hand and led her to a swing in the back part of the lawn.

"What's going on in your life, Jess?"

"I'm embarrassed to admit it, but you and my folks were right. I'm in no way suited for a career in law enforcement or criminal justice. That presents a problem. What am I going to do? About school this year? A job when I get out of school? I need to change majors which will extend my schooling by at least a year or two. My scholarship expires this year so any additional classes would have to come out of my pocket. I can't ask mom and dad to bail me out.

"And Callie, all of that has greatly wrecked my *hoped for* plans for us. How could I have been so mistaken about a career direction?"

"Have you ever had one of those career screening tests, Jesse?"

"No, but I'm going to check into that as soon as I can."

"Don't be so tough on yourself. Look at me. I never considered business as a career until this summer. You'll find something you're wired for ... something you will enjoy and do extremely well."

"You're not worried about us?"

"No, enough has happened in my short life to teach me that God causes all things to work for our good when we choose to love Him above all else. We just have to take it step by step and day by day."

"Pinch me, Callie. Is this real or am I dreaming?"

She playfully pinched his arm. "Oh, it's real, Jesse."

He wanted to take it easy, but he also wanted to kiss his girl again. About the time his lips touched hers, his stomach growled like a bear rousing from hibernation. Both laughed. "This growing boy didn't get his Cheerios this morning. Let's go break our fast."

As they were walking back to the house, Jesse questioned her about the new wheels. She told him Joseph arranged for her to get a really good deal. That was the truth -- just not all of it.

That thought lead her into the quagmire of other secrets not yet revealed. Her finances. Her engagement. Should she tell him? Did he need to know? Was she being dishonest with him? She remembered how David's secrets had wounded her, but this was different, wasn't it? She didn't have answers to those questions yet, but one thing she did know. She never wanted to hurt him again, and she knew there was potential for hurt inside both those secrets. Quiet seemed the best route to take at the moment.

Their days and time together were healing ... for both. Jesse brightened Callie's days with his sunshine and laughter, and Callie's presence resurrected Jesse's zest for life and living.

Callie appreciated Jesse's willingness to move slower than he wanted to in the relationship, because her emotions were running the gamut. There were times when she wondered if it wasn't too soon to be in a serious relationship with anyone, especially Jesse.

Their return to school threw both of them into overdrive. Football and changing career directions put a crunch on free time for Jesse. A screening test revealed he was an ideal candidate for a business or law degree. The legal field held no interest, so he enrolled in the Business

College. Then he opted for a heavy class load. Between that and football, they didn't have much of a social life but Callie saw that as a blessing. It gave her time to continue to deal and heal.

She was able to work in a business class. In addition she asked her folks to consider flying out for a weekend, take in a home game and meet Jesse and his family. Their approval was important to her.

The Adams threesome made it to the October matchup with Iowa. The Sooners won 35-16. Number eighty-five impressed the Virginia folks on and off the field. His parents commented on the balance Callie brought to Jesse and her parents were pleased to see the much needed levity he added to her life. Neither questioned his love for her and though it was obvious she cared for him, it was apparent that Jesse's attachment was stronger at this point.

Jesse borrowed his mom's station wagon to take them back to the airport. John pulled Callie aside before boarding. "Not only is Jesse a fine young man, Callie, he brings a light to your eyes that we haven't seen since you lost David. His love for you is obvious. I sense a reluctance in you and that's understandable, but at some point, you need to let go of the fear and dare to love again, Sweetheart."

She hugged her daddy with an air of grateful relief. "Thanks, Dad. He is a terrific guy and I am falling in love with him. But there are still times when the love David and I shared sweeps over me. That makes me feel guilty for loving Jesse and then when I'm with Jesse, I feel guilty for still loving David."

"I've not walked the path you are having to take, Callie, but I don't think those are unusual feelings. I'm confident the Lord and time will help you work through them. Be patient with yourself."

As her family was boarding the plane, Jesse put his arm around Callie's shoulders. She turned to face him and hugged him with a new depth of emotion.

"Hey, Girlfriend. Are you okay?"

"Yes, Jesse. I am!" She tiptoed and kissed him lightly on the cheek.

With a grin that turned her knees to noodles, he pointed to his lips. "I think you missed your target, Sweetheart." She kissed him on the lips ... and he returned the favor.

As they drove back to the ranch, Jesse was beside himself. He had the ring in his possession now and was only waiting for Callie to confirm what he prayed was true -- that she loved him. He was confident she did, but she had never spoken the words. Her folks' visit had released something inside her and his feet wanted to dance.

October and November passed and still the ring was in the box. He was hoping she would be wearing it before the holiday break. With a 10-2 record, the Sooners were headed to the Orange Bowl, January $2^{nd}$, and that would take a bite out of his break, plus Callie would be on the east coast. He might have to wait until the break was over. *What is her holdup?*

## Chapter 42

As the end of the semester and the holiday break neared, Callie approached Jesse. "Would you consider going home with me for the holidays? I know you have to prepare for the upcoming bowl game, but you do get a few days off. It would give you a good opportunity to get to know my family better and see where I grew up. And get this! Uncle Joseph has invited you to stay with him and shadow him at work the days the business is open. What do you think?"

Jesse seemed reluctant. "What about getting back to school for practice sessions before the game?"

"Uncle Joseph said he would arrange your flights in and out to suit your schedule."

"Let me think about it and talk to my folks. I'll let you know."

"You'll love Uncle Joseph, Jesse. He's easy to be around and folks who know say he has a brilliant business mind, and besides, we would be together."

His dimples deepened as his arms encircled her. "You know how to tempt a guy, don't you? Yeah, you might be incentive enough to go."

"I'd better be," she said as she reached up to kiss his cheek. "Let me know by tomorrow. Tickets need to be secured quickly."

"Excuse me, Girlfriend. You keep missing your target. I don't want any more of those brotherly cheek pecks." He tapped his lips. She stretched and kissed him soundly. "Hmm, now that's much better. Think I will call the folks tonight."

When he shared Callie's invitation with his mom, she urged him to go. "She's spent time on your home turf with us, Jesse. Her request indicates she is interested in moving the relationship forward. I don't think you can turn her down. I would think you'd want to spend as much time with her as possible. This has been a busy semester and quality time together has been scare for you two."

"Okay, I'll go. Thanks for your advice. Anybody flying out for the bowl game?"

"I think Roger and one of his friends have made plans to be there. Your dad and I can't make it, but he has rented the community center and invited an army to join us. You'll probably hear us. We'll see you after the holidays."

He got his days cleared with the coach the next day and alerted Callie. Joseph secured the tickets. Callie flew home a few days before Jesse could get away from football practice. When he did fly in, she and John met him at the airport. John dropped them off at the dealership. After a brief introduction and chit-chat, Joseph handed Jesse a key ring and pointed to a new Chevy Monte Carlo. "One set fits the car and the other fits the front door of the house. Consider both yours this week."

"Wow! Thanks Mr. Henderson."

Callie showed him around the physical plant of the dealership, so he would be familiar with the layout and know a couple of folks when he showed up for work. Then she served as tour guide of the area as they drove toward Henderson Hills.

"Now I know why you love this place, Callie. It is wildly beautiful. I'm banking on the predicted snow, so we can check out the slopes at Wintergreen. I think I'm going to enjoy this little trip!"

As they turned up the lane to Henderson Hills, Jesse stopped the car. "Wow! This is some place, Callie. It looks like a painting."

"Yeah, I've had the same thought at times."

"Get a load of that hacienda! I thought our house was big and rambling, but this ... Look at those stables! Joseph's pockets must be deep."

That statement and thought made Callie uncomfortable. Should she tell him? It still didn't seem like the right time. She was beginning to wonder if the right time would ever come. His attention turned to something else and she let the subject pass without comment.

They set his suitcase inside the house, checked on the horses and then headed to Callie's place for the evening. Her folks welcomed him graciously. A couple of hours later, he told Callie that Carla reminded him of somebody he knew, but he couldn't figure out who it was.

She hugged him. "Keep your eye on her; you'll figure it out."

When it was time for him to leave for the night, Callie walked him to his car. "Can you find your way back to Uncle Joseph's place?"

"Sure, but I'd rather stay at your place." He pulled her close.

"Are you uncomfortable about staying with Uncle Joseph, Jesse? If you are, we can move you to our guest room."

"No, I'm being selfish. I just want to be close to you. Seeing this beautiful part of the country and getting to know your folks are perks. And I appreciate Joseph's offer to shadow him a few days, but you are the main attraction, Callie. Surely you know that." His kiss erased any doubts she might have had.

Callie was falling for this zany, sweet, gorgeous man and his kisses were beginning to leave her weak-kneed and a stomach filled with butterflies. "Jesse Collins, we're going to have to set some boundaries if you keep kissing me like that."

"So I'm finally getting through to you? Callie girl, I keep trying to convince you that I love you."

She wanted to tell him that she loved him but memories of the love David shared with her this time last year were surfacing. She tiptoed and kissed him lightly on his cheek.

He cleared his throat and pointed to his lips. She kissed him softly. "I've never deserved your love, Jesse. Never." Tears began slowly rolling down her cheeks. She hugged him tightly and started to walk back towards the house.

A strong hand grabbed her wrist and gently pulled her back around. "Cal, we've had this talk before. For the life of me I can't figure out why you keep insisting you don't deserve my love. What makes you say such a thing?"

"I played with your heart to soothe my own personal wounds and that was so wrong, Jess."

"Well, you're not playing with it now, are you?"

"No, it's just that I can't stand the thought of ever hurting you again. What if I do, Jesse?"

"The only way you're going to hurt me now is to walk out of my life. You don't plan to do that, do you, Callie?"

"No, Jesse, I don't."

"Then I never want to hear that statement again. Okay?"

"Okay." As a lone tear trailed down her cheek, she put her hands on the sides of his face and softly kissed one cheek and then the other. Before he could point to his lips, she lightly brushed his lips with hers. "Goodnight, Mr. Collins. I'm falling for you."

All the way to Joseph's he replayed that conversation. *Why can't she just come out and tell me she loves me? It would have been a perfect time to give her this ring I keep carrying around. Sometimes that woman frustrates my frustrations and confuses my confusion.*

The Henderson house was quiet but well lit when he arrived. It was late and Joseph had gone to bed. He found a note explaining that his room was downstairs with his suitcase in front of the door.

As he walked through the house, it suddenly occurred to him that he had never seen a picture of David. There were several scattered around and just as many of Callie and David. Seeing the two of them together brought their relationship into clearer focus. They were a handsome couple. David had dark features like Callie.

His accommodations would rival any five star hotel. The furnishings were first-class and the design eye catching. He could get used to this kind of life. First he had to finish school and find a job.

The next morning as he headed to the kitchen to grab a bite, an 8 x 10 framed photo on a table in the den caught his attention. Joseph spotted him staring at it and told him it was David and Callie's official engagement photo. It was a profile shot and they had eyes only for each other.

Why should that surprise or bother him? It did both. He kept reminding himself that they were engaged when he met Callie and she was certainly in love with the man. Why shouldn't they look at each other that way? Was he jealous that she had loved someone before him? Surely not. Was he just now facing that reality? Probably so. In the past

David had been just a name, a figment, a two-timing jerk. Now he had a face, a rich dad, and a home -- plus a wife. The wife part is what really bothered him.

He tried to erase that picture from his mind, but it was already etched in his memory bank and all day it kept flashing images at his heart. Was he jealous of David or upset with Callie for marrying a cheater? He decided it wasn't either or, it was both.

Another question emerged. Did Callie's proclamations of her love for David and her yet undeclared love for him have a bearing on why her relationship with David bothered him so much? It didn't help.

Looking back he realized that was a part of her life that she had held close. Maybe she knew he hadn't been ready to deal with it. Truthfully he wasn't coping with it well even now. David might be gone, but his influence and impact were not.

Jesse had noticed tears in Callie's eyes several times. He was pretty sure they were for David. The anniversaries of the accident, their marriage and his death were only days away. How was he supposed to deal with that? He didn't know, so he stayed silent.

His counterpart had learned the hard way that life is precious and uncertain and that every day is a gift and people are the treasures. Callie did love and treasure Jesse, but memories of David were popping up uninvited. That was making her time with Jesse testing, especially with the anniversaries so close.

She had noticed Jesse's discomfort every time David's name was mentioned, so she did her grieving alone or with her family. David's memories were here and his grave was close.

Why hadn't she considered the timing of Jesse's trip with the events of last year? She was actually grateful he would be flying out before Christmas, not because she didn't care; but because he didn't understand.

Jesse and Callie spent all their spare time together. They went horseback riding a couple of times on what he declared to be well-bred and pricey horses. They worked in a ski outing and took in several celebrations of the season. Although they were enjoying being together, both were secretly fighting their own battles.

The day before Jesse had to head back to school, he and Joseph were invited to join the Adams family for dinner. Carla was in a talkative mood the entire evening which meant her filtering system was turned off again. She was trying to keep Jesse engaged in conversation. "Hey, Jesse, how do you like Callie's Blazer?"

"Kind of classy for a struggling college girl but I hear Joseph got her a good deal."

"Well, I don't know about that, but I do know that Callie isn't a poor struggling student. She's loaded! David left her oodles of money and she can buy anything she wants. Didn't she tell you?"

Jesse's countenance clouded immediately. He looked around the table waiting for someone to correct Carla. All heads turned to Callie. His gaze caught hers and he knew Carla spoke truth. He responded with both shock and anger in his voice. "No, she didn't, Carla. Thanks for letting me know."

He excused himself from the table and walked out the door into the chill of winter. Too late fifteen year old Carla realized she had spoken without thinking. She looked at Callie, "I'm truly sorry, Sis. I didn't know he didn't know."

"Well, he knows now and I guess I've got some explaining to do. Pray, folks. This may not go down well." She grabbed her coat and his.

He was sitting on the porch swing shivering. She handed him his coat and noted his body wasn't the only thing chilled at this moment.

"When did you plan to tell me, Callie?"

"I've wanted to tell you, Jess, but it never seemed like the appropriate time. I'm sorry you had to find out this way." She sat on the swing beside him. "When Uncle Joseph told me about David's finances the night after the funeral, I was as surprised then as you are now. I knew his dad made a good living but I never dreamed David was rich. His money came from his Mom's folks but he never said a word about it. Except for their home, they don't live like wealthy folks and they sure don't talk about it."

"Didn't the rings give you a clue?"

"No, Jesse, remember? They were his mom's."

"You've not been honest with me, Callie. That hurts. Don't you trust me?"

"It's never been about not trusting you, Jesse. It's been about not wanting to ever hurt you again."

"So tell me now."

"Oh, okay ... Well, I've been left with a rather ... uh ... large bank account ... and some ... sizable assets, Jesse ..."

She paused as the eerie sound of a lone coyote pierced the silence of the night.

"That's it? A fat bank account and sizable assets?"

"Well, not exactly."

"There's more?" His voice and agitation levels shot up a notch.

"Jess, please don't get upset. Yes, there is more. When David graduated, his dad transferred forty percent of the shares of the dealership into his name." She knew he had already figured that one out. "Those shares have been transferred to me."

Jesse jumped out of the swing and turned to face her. "Are you telling me that you own forty percent of the business I have been working for? Have I been working for you?"

"Hmmm ... I never looked at it that way ..."

"Any other surprises hidden in that vault of yours, rich keeper of secrets?" He was not even trying to hide his anger at this point.

"As a matter of fact there are, but I can't see what good it would do to tell you now. You're already upset and I remember what your tempter looks like when you lose control. I have no desire to experience that again."

Jesse's response was demanding. "Oh, you need to tell me, Callie. If our future together means anything to you, I'm suggesting you tell it all. Do you own the New York Yankees or an island in the Caribbean? The magnitude of your surprises would wreck the Richter scale. I'm asking you to come clean. Spit it all out now."

"Jesse, I don't understand why you're getting so upset over something I didn't plan and had no control over. It just happened and I'm sorry I didn't tell you sooner. Your reaction is proving that I had reason to question how you would respond. Our relationship has always been challenged by complications. I just didn't want to throw anything else in the mix."

"Well, it's in the mix now and it undeniably puts us back in a relationship challenged by complications. Out with it, Callie."

"I don't think now is a good time to discuss this, Jesse, but I'm learning you have a stubborn streak as well as a temper." With a sigh of giving up, Callie continued. "I've told you part of this one before …"

"Part of it, Callie?" he interrupted. "You have purposely deceived me? Dishonesty and deception destroy relationships, at least they should. I guess you forgot all that when you agreed to marry David. Well, I won't forget."

"Okay, Jess, if you will quit interrupting, I'll tell you." She took a deep breath trying to speak calmly instead of react to his anger. "Another reason David wanted me to marry him was his dad. He knew Uncle Joseph would be left alone. I am the only family he has, Jesse. You've been around us. He treats me like his daughter. He has made me his beneficiary as well."

Jesse didn't speak. He paced the length of the porch and back before throwing his barbs. "That means that the house I've been staying in will be yours one day … and oh, don't forget all that farm land and horses. And the business I've been working for … *all of it* will one day belong to you! You don't need a husband, Callie. You just need an accountant and a lawyer."

"What do you want me to do, Jess? I didn't marry David for his wealth. I married him … because I loved him. Does being rich make me suddenly unlovable?"

He walked to the edge of the porch and turned his back to her. Callie knew at this point that she had to be completely honest with Jesse … even if it meant losing him.

"Jesse, there's more. I wasn't sure I would ever tell you the story behind our marriage. Maybe I've been wrong withholding that as well. My excuse was that I was trying to protect you. I feared the truth would tear us apart -- and it may, but starting tonight, Jesse Collins, there will be no more secrets on my part. I'm telling it all."

He turned to face her. Finally the truth was going to come out and he was pretty sure he wasn't going to like this saga any better than the rich widow tale. He moved back to the swing and waited for her to continue.

"I told you when I left for the break last year that I wanted to find resolution to the confusion over my love for David and my feelings for you. Much happened those days and weeks and all led to the early morning hours of the New Year when David put his engagement ring back on my finger. We were engaged before his accident, Jesse."

A weight began to crush his heart as his greatest fear just became his worst nightmare. The money news was small change compared to this mother lode she'd exposed. He was fighting every human instinct in his body in order to keep his voice down. "Are you telling me that if the accident had not happened that you and David would now be married and I wouldn't be here tonight?"

"Yes."

He jumped off the porch and walked to the edge of the driveway. She walked quietly and stood beside him.

"Jesse, I'm sorry for all the pain I keep causing you."

He looked at her with the aloofness of a casual acquaintance. "Obviously, you don't consider it any of my business, but I'm curious. How rich are you, Callie? Are we talking six digits or seven?"

"I'm sorry it matters to you."

"Honesty is what matters to me. You are a very wealthy lady, aren't you?"

"If you must know ... yes, Jesse, I am. It was an unexpected gift prompted by David's love. And I refuse to be ashamed of either of those facts."

That nugget of truth took his breath away. "Like I said before, Callie. Your surprises are off the charts! How am I supposed to deal with all of this?"

"The money hasn't changed who I am, Jess, but it certainly seems to be having an impact on you. It's not just the marriage part, is it?"

He began walking back to the house. "No, both of them are unsettling to me right now. Is there anything else your sudden honesty might prompt you to reveal?"

"Yes, actually there are two more things." He had stopped at the porch steps. She moved to the first step so she could look in his eyes. "After you ranked so high in business on your screening test, I called Uncle Joseph and told him about your situation with careers and having to postpone graduation due to changing majors. It was his idea to get you here this break. He knew that I cared for you. He wanted to meet you and see how you would do in the business arena."

She placed her hand on his crossed arms and he jerked as though she had touched him with a branding iron. "He's excited, Jesse. He likes you as a person and sees great potential in you as a partner."

"Sees me as a partner? That's makes no sense, Callie."

"Well, that involves the other thing I haven't told you yet." She waited until their eyes locked. "I love you, Jesse Collins, and I want to marry you. If we married, I'd give you that forty percent and you would be a business partner with Uncle Joseph. He would eventually back out and give it all to you."

Jesse was stunned and Callie took advantage of the moment. "So I guess now the question is -- can you deal with the truth I've shared tonight? I loved David. I married him. He left me a wealthy widow. I love you, Jesse. I want to marry you. I want to share David's blessings with you. His dad wants to bless us as well. Can you accept my past with David and my love for you now?"

Jesse moved away from her and sat on the swing again. He put his head in his hands and didn't make a move or say a word for a long time. Finally he pulled a ring box out of his coat pocket. "I've been carrying this around waiting to hear those three words from you for weeks and now that I have, I find I can't put it on your finger. I don't trust you anymore, Callie. You have kept some very significant information from me and I feel betrayed. The harsh truth is I've always played second fiddle to David and even now he comes out the winner. That hurts."

Callie felt a surge of anger move through her. "Jesse, my love for David has never been a secret. You always knew you were involved in a triangle. My mistake was encouraging you while shutting David out. Our lives would have crossed in classes and with Heather and Kirk, but I should have kept it at the friendship level. I didn't and for that

I'm sorry. I've caused you great pain, but Jesse, you are not completely innocent in all of this. You have been relentlessly persistent.

"If David were alive, I could understand the second fiddle thoughts, but his chair is empty and I should know. I was holding him in my arms when he vacated it." The tear flow broke through.

"It's empty, Jesse, and I'm inviting you to be first in my life, not second. You will be my second love but you can now occupy the first chair. That's all I can offer. I don't want you to walk away, but I've learned that love is not only something that happens, but more than that ... it is a choice. I choose to love you. You are free to accept or refuse that love."

"I have loved you for over two years, Callie. That certainly involved a strong physical attraction and desire, but it was much more and you know that. As you know from experience, trust destroyed is not quickly regained. Right now I can't tell you how these newest revelations are going to impact our relationship. I need time. Would you tell Joseph that I'm ready to head back to the house? I think he and I have much to discuss."

"I do understand the pain of being deceived and experiencing betrayal, Jesse. I'm deeply sorry to be the source of that kind of pain in you. I pray one day you will forgive me. I'll send Uncle Joseph out." She leaned over and kissed his cheek. There was no pointing to the lips this time.

Joseph and Jesse did talk -- all the way home and late into the night. Joseph confirmed all that Callie had told him. Jesse listened but said little.

Callie drove him to the airport early the next morning. Jesse was quiet. He had asked for time. She would honor that. He had spent much time waiting for her to work through different challenges. She would be patient. Conversation was almost nil.

As they neared the airport, Jesse told her that he not only needed time, he needed space. He wanted to put their relationship on hold. No dates, no calls, no contacts. He was shutting her out. She remembered being on the other side of a shutout.

Jesse asked her to drop him off and leave. After he retrieved his suitcase from the trunk, his eyes swept over her and then locked with hers. His look housed such a tormenting mixture of love and loss that it brought a flood of tears to Callie. She knew he was quietly dismissing her from his life. In spite of him, she moved forward and lightly kissed him on his lips and whispered, "I love you, Jesse. Take care." He turned and walked away without a word.

# Chapter 43

The plane ride home was the loneliest time in Jesse's life. Callie's declaration of love was cancelled out by her secrets and deception. He couldn't deal with that. He had made the choice to shut her out of his life. Now he had to find a way to get her out of his heart and off his mind.

He poured his hurt and anger into the practices and preparing for the upcoming bowl game. That only served to increase his frustrations. It was going to take more than that to eradicate her memory. He needed to be more decisive.

His folks were crushed when he told them it was over between him and Callie. Step one in Callie removal. The night before the bowl game, he tore his list into shreds and buried it in his waste can in the hotel room. Step two in Callie removal.

The Sooners lost their bowl game. It was an emotional time for all the seniors, but Jesse had a double load to deal with. He played his worst game … ever … because all he could think about was that his rich ex-girlfriend was watching. He hoped she was as miserable as he was.

In Lynchburg, Joseph had joined her family to watch the game. Watching Jesse was a bitter sweet experience … for all of them. Callie had surrendered their relationship to God.

"Have you heard from Jesse since he left, Callie?" Joseph asked.

"No, Uncle Joseph, I haven't. If he can't come to terms with David's part in my life, then we will have no future. When he left, he was not even close. All I know to do is pray and wait."

Callie Henderson wept as the loss of two loves tore at her heart. Both during the Christmas season and the beginning of a New Year. Again it was the manger that had brought her back to God's love. She thanked God for Jesus ... and David. She prayed for Jesse. She refused to live in the *Land of If* this time. She would face her wrong choices and trust the Lord for the healing of both losses. She knew that neither death nor misunderstanding would separate her from God and His love. She was going to rest in that ... through the pain and tears.

# Chapter 44

Callie flew back to school broken, and yet at peace. She refused to discuss the details of hers and Jesse's breakup with Heather or Kirk.

Two weeks became three weeks and three became four. A month became two and then three. She never saw Jesse. OU was big enough to avoid or miss anyone you didn't purposely want to see. Just as David waited for her to forgive him and trust him again, now she was waiting for Jesse to forgive and trust her again. And if he didn't ...

Although her relationship with Jesse had fallen apart, she continued to experience the reality of being pursued and loved by God as much as she had been by David. God was fast becoming her best friend.

Kirk and Heather were bewildered. Heather had tried to bring up the subject before with no success. After four months of silence, she confronted Callie again. "Roomie, Kirk is very concerned about Jesse's behavior since you two broke up. I'm concerned about you. Losing David last year and Jesse this year cannot be easy. We've been friends for four years, Callie. What happened?"

Callie began to cry. The news about Jesse was disturbing. She slowly related the events of their visit to Virginia. "Callie, you've got more secrets than the CIA. So he's upset because he found out you are rich?"

"Heather, I had not been honest with Jesse about the money or my engagement to David before the accident. I think the money issue bothered him, the engagement rattled him and my dishonesty about both of them was the final blow. Three strikes and Jesse walked out of my life with an engagement ring in his pocket."

"He bought an engagement ring for you and then wouldn't give it to you? That's sad. You two have had a tough time." Heather paused as though considering how much to reveal. "Kirk thinks you should know that Jesse has been spending time with a cute blond named Emma, who's known for being on the wild side. Kirk said he has smelled alcohol lately and Jesse is not keeping decent hours. You've heard nothing from him since December 24th?"

With fresh tears and new pain, Callie shook her head. "Zero! I've not seen or heard from Jesse since the day I dropped him off at the airport. I've wanted to call or go see him a dozen times, but what would I say that hasn't already been said?"

She called Jesse's mom that night. Jesse had only shared with them that the problems between them had something to do with David still being in the picture. Callie asked if he mentioned seeing anyone. Margaret admitted that he brought a friend home just last weekend. "He's trying real hard to get you out of his heart, Callie. I don't think he will succeed. If I know my son, he'll come to his senses sooner or later. We are praying it won't be too late. He's not making smart choices. Dean and I are very concerned."

"For the record, Margaret, I love your son and am willing and ready to marry him. He's struggling with my love for and marriage to David and the fact that all of David's wealth is now mine. I haven't heard from him since the day I dropped him off at the airport in Roanoke."

"Oh, thank you for sharing that! Don't give up on him, Callie. That boys loves you. There's hope."

They hung up and Callie wept ... and prayed for Jesse.

Soon afterwards, Jesse took a call from his mom. Margaret told him about talking with Callie. "Son, you need to forgive that girl for not being perfect and for loving someone else before she ever met you. She's yours for the asking, Jesse. Don't be prideful and stubborn. We love you, but you are making a huge mistake and you know it. We are praying for merciful misery that will bring you to your senses ... and your knees."

"Gee, thanks, Mom. More misery is just what I need. I'll talk to you later." And Jesse hung up.

He was misery personified. In the process of trying to eradicate Callie from his heart, he met Emma, who was an enticing distraction with an outgoing personality and an exquisite body. With promises to help him forget *what's her name*, she quickly broke down his resistance and crossed all his boundaries.

Problem was that Emma's way of life was addicting and he knew he was moving in that direction. And though he had given up on God as well as Callie, it seemed that God wasn't giving up on him. His guilt and misery levels kept increasing.

Even if he could forgive Callie, at this point she could never forgive him. She had been through this other woman thing with David and he was confident she wasn't going there again. Maybe that's what he was unconsciously trying to do. Hurt her and drive her away. He didn't love Emma and had no plans to marry her. Surviving the last weeks of school was his goal and then both women would be gone.

On the other side of campus, Callie made a decision. "Heather, do you think Kirk would do me a favor?"

"Sure!" Heather jumped at the chance to help out.

"Will you ask him to set up something so I can meet with Jesse without his knowing ahead of time it is me? It's time for one last face to face encounter."

"We will arrange it."

Kirk invited Jesse to an end of the year party at Lake Thunderbird State Park Friday night. He asked him to wait at the pavilion closest to the entrance. Jesse asked if he could bring Emma. Kirk told him no.

Jesse was there on time but not one other person had shown up. *Am I in the wrong place or did I get the wrong date?*

About the time he considered leaving, he saw another vehicle approaching. It looked like Kirk's. Good. It was. Another person was in the truck but he couldn't tell who it was. Kirk got out and started walking towards Jesse. The other person stayed in the truck.

"Hey, what's going on? We are the only ones who've shown up here. Am I at the wrong place?"

"You are at the right place, Roomie, and no one else is going to show up. It's just us. Have a seat, Jess. I've got some things I need to say. So sit tight and listen."

Jesse was rather stunned, but since Kirk was the top weight lifter on the team and hadn't been too happy with him lately, he complied.

"Since your return from Virginia, you've changed, and not for the better. Somewhere back in that state you lost yourself. This new Jesse is one messed up dude. His brain is fried and his heart is becoming stone.

"What happened that would cause you to walk away from one of the finest girls I've ever known and if you will admit it, the only one you've ever loved. You are not being fair to Emma either, Jesse. She's not Callie and she can't and won't replace her in your heart. You are acting like a first class jerk and nobody knows why. Your sorry excuses stink as badly as your behavior.

"Another thing. There is a young lady in my truck who would like some private time with you. I'm going to hang around to be sure she gets it, so don't think about running or being rude. I've been looking for a good reason to take you down. You're going to listen and hopefully you're going to be honest with yourself and her. You owe her that.

"And for the record, I'll be taking her home tonight no matter what happens between you. If you aren't any smarter when we leave than you are right now, I promise you there is some lucky guy out there who will recognize the treasure that you have discarded and win her heart.

"Jess, I've envied what you two had. In fact, seeing you and Callie encouraged me to make my own list. And I've got a news flash for you. Your girl meets a lot of them, so if you are fool enough to stay away too long you might find some competition you recognize. Problem with that is ... she loves you. I'm going to get her, and I'm going to be keeping my eyes on you. You'd better behave."

Jesse was dumbfounded. He had been set up. That was Callie in the truck! And exactly what was Kirk implying? He watched him help Callie out of the truck as though she was royalty. And the king brought the queen to the court jester.

As Callie removed her hand, Kirk turned to her. "Callie, I don't care what happens tonight, I'm taking you home. Take your time. I'll be waiting."

Kirk turned and walked back to his truck. Jesse and Callie stood staring at each other. Callie heard the inner whisper. *Callie, My love is a love of choice, surrender and sacrifice. Unconditional. Nothing less.*

"Hi, Jess."

"Hi, Cal."

The electricity between them could have lit up the park. One touch would have proven that. "I'm sorry for using Kirk to get you here. I kept waiting for you to make some kind of contact. I gave up. I'd like some answers before you walk out of my life."

"Such as?"

"You asked me to be honest. I was. I'm asking the same of you. For starters, do you still love me?"

Jesse turned and began pacing around in the pavilion. "Truth? You want to hear the truth? Okay. Yes, I still love you, Callie. That's my problem. I shut you out of my life hoping that I could get you out of my heart. I've tried, but I've had no success thus far. I have met someone who convinced me she could help me forget you. Her name is Emma. I judged David for his unfaithfulness and now I make him look like a saint."

Callie wasn't prepared for that truth. She grabbed a pole to steady herself. Tears began to crowd her eyes. "Oh Jess, not you!"

"Yeah, me. Being the poor, good guy didn't pay off. You married the rich, bad one. So I've been winging it and have found there are some pleasures in the world. Emma is not only fun to be with, but she makes me feel like a man. Believe it or not, Callie, I'm her number one, not number two man. That's a good feeling after being your number two for the last two plus years."

"Makes you feel like a man, Jesse? What kind of screwed logic and distorted truth is that? There is a huge difference between being a male and being a man. Having sex doesn't make you a man. It just means your hormones are functioning and you've indulging your flesh.

"You may still love me, Jess, but you haven't forgiven me, have you? Unforgiveness sentences us to a prison of our own making with bitterness as our cellmate."

"I can identify with being in a prison, but I don't know how to get out, Callie. I'm tormented by the fact that if David were still alive you'd be his wife."

"Ah, yes. The illusive *Land of If.* I'm well acquainted with living there. It's a place that is based on what isn't true; therefore, it has to be based on lies. It's a place that robs us of our peace and hope, a place that destroys our faith and has as its goal the death of our relationship with God and others. Many times I despaired of my own life in that land.

"Some of the last words I heard from David's mouth before his accident was that he surrendered all three of us to God's will. Do you know how much I have struggled with that prayer? Yet it was that prayer that helped me walk away from the *Land of If.* Many die there, Jess. Don't be a casualty.

"Sweet Jesse, do you know that God loves and wants a relationship with you more than you have loved and wanted one with me? David, lust and booze are not your problems. Your lack of an intimate relationship with God is. And until you grab hold of that truth and Him, then none of your other relationships will ever be right … for any length of time. And the temporary pleasures of sin that you use to medicate your pain will pull you into your own personal nightmare called addictions. For the sake of those you love and yourself, don't go there.

"And in case I never get another chance, I want you to know the truth about this David you have self-righteously judged the last two plus years. The first time he asked me to marry him, he was struggling with sexual temptations and purity and was following the advice of Paul about marrying rather than burn. I didn't think I was ready for marriage, so I said no. That's when Josie happened.

"His brokenness led him to the One who loved all of us even while we were still in our sins. He wept his way into the arms of that loving, forgiving God and while I rejected him, he found a Love that would never turn him away.

"He was learning to live out of that love the second time he asked me to marry him. He didn't beg, push or plead. He pursued with my needs in mind, not his, and his heart won mine the second time around. His ring went back on my finger and within an hour the unthinkable happened.

"The third time he asked me to marry him had absolutely nothing to do with him and everything to do with me. Knowing that his days were limited, he asked me to marry him so he could provide for my future.

"After we married, Jesse, he reminded me of your love for me. He knew that by blessing me that he was enriching you as well ... and yet he did it. What kind of love does that, Jesse? What kind of man gives his wife to another man on his death bed and then opens the windows of heaven and rains financial blessings all over both of them and any future generations?

"That was the kind of unselfish love that won me, Jesse. Thanks to his example, I've been learning to live loved by my Heavenly Father and learning to love others like He loves me." Callie stood up straight, drew in a deep breath and moved into his personal space. She placed a hand on his crossed arms. He visibly softened this time. "And that is how I choose to love you tonight."

Tears began to stream down her cheeks. "Jesse Collins, I make a choice ... to forgive you for your involvement with Emma. I pray that you confess your sins to God ... and her, repent and then seek God's love and accept his forgiveness."

Keeping her eyes fixed on his, she continued, "I free you ... from our relationship tonight. You can walk away without any guilt or feelings of obligation towards me. You owe me nothing, Jesse. My life has been made richer by knowing and being loved by you."

Her desire to hug him forced her to move out of his space. "This is not easy for me, Jesse." She reached in her pocket and pulled out a tissue to wipe the tears that continued to flow. "I love you ... and offer you my love again tonight. If you walk away, I believe that God has someone else in mind. If your choice is Emma, then love her like God loves you. Quit using her."

Jesse was now fighting his own tears but offered no response.

"With God's help, I choose to love you ... to forgive you ... and to release you. What happens next is up to you."

Callie waited a few minutes then turned and walked away.

The minute Kirk saw her turn to leave, he headed toward her. As he reached for her hand, she leaned into him and went weak. He put his arm around her and helped her back to his truck. As he was getting in the driver's side, he saw Jesse walking toward them. He met and stopped him before he reached Callie.

"You've had your chance. I'm taking her home. Go see Emma. Go do anything you want to do, but leave her alone. And when you get back to the room tonight, be very quiet. Right now, Jesse, I'm fighting a strong urge to beat some sense into you."

Jesse walked to his truck and drove away.

Callie was so still and quiet that Kirk was concerned. "You okay, Cal?"

"No, but I will be. I just need time. Thank you for tonight, Kirk. I owe you." She was hurting but she realized she wasn't devastated.

"Friends don't charge for favors, Callie."

"Good, because I have another one to ask. Could we ride around for a while? I need some time to let tonight sink in."

"Sure, do you want to go anywhere special?"

"I'd like to get on one of those sailboats and take a long trip, but I guess riding around will have to do."

"You've got it." He drove and let the quiet work its way through her.

Half an hour and twenty-five miles later, Callie asked, "Where is your home, Kirk?"

"Bristol, as in Tennessee."

"Hey, that's not too far from my hometown."

"I've known that for quite a while."

"What are you doing when you get back home?"

"Going to work with my dad in the family business. I understand the David's in life, Callie. I'm one of them."

They spent a couple of hours sharing and getting to know each other better and then he took her back to the dorm.

After that night, Kirk began to show up at meal times. She was grateful for his companionship. He added no stress and made no demands. He was just there. They made plans to make the trip back east together.

Kirk smiled as he shared about making sure Jesse was aware of every minute he and Callie were spending together, including his plans to follow her home and visit if she'd agree. He said Jesse never commented, but he had quit coming in drunk and did break up with Emma. Callie was relieved.

Callie called her parents and told them she wasn't walking for graduation. They didn't question her reasons. They were relieved that Kirk was following her back to Bristol.

Callie's four years at the University of Oklahoma came to an end; and Shelby, Callie and Kirk headed toward the sunrise. They spent the first night in a nice hotel. Kirk and Callie rested in Nashville for an hour when they dropped off Shelby, but decided to push on. Kirk followed Callie all the way home. Her grateful folks insisted he spend the night in their guest room. They were impressed with her rather large, but gentle friend.

Before Kirk left, he asked permission to stay in contact. Callie agreed but reminded him that friendship was all she could offer. He smiled. "You'll be hearing from me, Friend."

# CHAPTER 45

Callie didn't have to report to work until next Monday, so she and sixteen year old Carla took a few days to get her four years of accumulated belongings sorted, put away or ready for the Goodwill drop-off. She had one item to add to her treasure chest. A Sooners' team football. Maybe one day she'd package it up and send it back to Jesse's folks, but not today.

Determined to live fully today without regrets over her yesterdays, Callie headed for the local shopping center to purchase some needed professional outfits for her new job. Memories of Ella and David followed her and thoughts of Jesse weren't far behind. *Lord, thank you for the treasured relationships in my life. You are my number one treasure!*

As she neared the entrance to one of the department stores, she noticed an attractive pen on the pavement, picked it up and dropped it in her purse. After browsing through a couple of stores, she went home with three new outfits.

She was showing off her new finds to Beth when Carla stormed into the den in a frantic search. "What are you looking for, Carla?" Beth asked.

"Ah, Mom, I can't find my pen. I must have left it in here last night." Beth and Callie knew the pen could well be hiding with the other three or four she had misplaced recently and just smiled.

Callie reached into her purse and pulled out the parking lot pen. "Here, use this one."

"Gee, thanks, Sis." And away she went.

Callie was in her room hanging up her new outfits when Carla barreled in. "Hey, this is a really nice pen. Where did you get it?"

Callie told her the story.

"Did you noticed the word imprinted on it?"

"No, I just saw it and put it in my purse. What's the word?"

"*Treasured*. There's lighter print in the background but I can't read it."

"Treasured!"

Carla handed her the pen and left the room. Sure enough, in bold black letters was the word, *Treasured*. Callie held the pen under her desk lamp and read the lighter print on the pen. *Deut. 26:18. You are a dearly held treasure.*

*That's you, Daughter. You are a dearly held treasure.*

*Me? Treasured? A dearly held treasure?* Waterworks broke loose. She read the pen again. *A dearly held treasure!* An intangible Presence filled her room ... and her heart. She closed her door and her room became their secret chamber. Praise mingled with tears.

*Finding out that You pursue us with the passion of all the lovers of all the ages has messed up my theology, Lord. Learning that Your love for us has been woven throughout creation, was born in a manger, nailed to a cross and defied death in order to open the door to a personal and intimate relationship with You has turned my life upside down. But to be treasured by You? That possibility blows my mind! Is it really true?*

*Yes, Callie. You and all my children are treasures ... dearly held by Me.*

Tears were flowing freely and a gentle warmth began to slowly permeate her body. She smiled and rested in His Presence. She loved God hugs, but this one ...

*I am my Beloved's treasure ... and He is mine.* She loved and was loved. She treasured and was treasured ... by her number One Love and Treasure.

A gentle knock indicating the evening meal was ready revealed that she had lingered. With worshipful amazement, she knelt by the trunk and added God's love token. *Abba, how does one fully comprehend what it means to be treasured by You? You lack nothing and own it all and yet say to us, Your children, that we are dearly held treasures? Let that amazing truth become reality in me.*

She shared her parking lot pen story with her family that evening and three days later her dad announced that he had located the manufacturer of her pen. "Are you ready for this, Callie? Your pen was manufactured in the United Kingdom and currently it is not being sold on the market. What do you think about that news?"

Fresh tears began to trail down her cheeks. "Oh, Dad! For me that is Heaven's *amen*. Whether God used a human or an angel to deliver that pen I know not. What matters is the message ... that He loves and treasures me ... all of us.

"I'm beginning to understand that all of His directions for living, guidelines for relationships and boundaries are rooted in His heart of Love. Their purpose is to bless and protect, not deprive and deny. He knows the fallout of selfish living and points us to a better way ... unselfish Love."

John was watching his number one daughter process this new revelation. "Yes, Callie, and too many times by our own choices we declare that we think we are wiser than this God who made us, died for us, loves and treasures us. How foolish! And even then, His love never changes. He waits for our messes and the circumstances that surround us to turn our attention to Him. He never quits loving us. He never gives up. Love never dies."

For the rest of the week, she willingly took time to shut out the world and close herself in with her Beloved. Every day her perspective on life and living was changing. By the time Monday came, Callie was eager to get to work. She was fully trusting her Number One Love and Treasure with all of her todays and tomorrows and that included her loss of David and Jesse's rejection.

She went directly to Joseph's office. He welcomed her with a warm hug. They talked awhile and then he took her down the hall and stopped at the door to David's former office. The sign had been changed. It now read, *Callie Adams Henderson, VP of Henderson Enterprises*. Will these tears ever dry up? Joseph handed her a key and urged her to check out her new office. He walked back to his.

There was an excitement as she opened the door to her new future. She walked in marveling at the new decor. Somebody knew her taste. It was inviting, yet professional. As she turned to her left, she noticed the private restroom. *Nice perk!* Dead center was a beautiful walnut desk and matching bookshelf area. To her right was a cozy sitting area, complete with love seat, table and chair. More walnut bookshelves served as room dividers. In a corner nook was a small kitchenette. All she needed was a bed and she could live here. She left her door open and ambled to her desk. It was a smaller version of the massive one in Joseph's office. Her chair was plush and inviting. She gave it a try. As she lifted her eyes to survey the room, she noticed movement near her door. A figure stepped out of the shadows. "Jesse?"

"Hi Callie," spoke a man whose whole demeanor had changed. This was definitely gorgeous Jesse, but not the Jesse of their last encounter. He moved toward her and dropped into one of the chairs in front of her desk. Neither spoke.

Jesse broke the silence. "You look great, Callie."

Her mind was trying to explain this moment to her heart. Her heart dared to hope and tears were rolling again.

"Jess, what are you doing here?"

"Asking for another chance."

Her tears quit playing follow the leader and began chasing each other. "I'm listening."

"Callie, I have made some stupid choices and arrived at some dumb conclusions because of my pride and self-righteous ego. I had been fairly confident that I would win your love after David's unfaithfulness. I thought it was just a matter of time. Learning that you had accepted his ring again ripped me apart. Why would you choose a guy who had cheated on you over one who had stayed in the background and loved you through it all? I was hurt and furious. I felt like you and God had failed me, so I gave up on both of you.

"That set me up for Emma. She proved there are pleasures in our sinning but the guilt tormented me. I drank to drown the guilt, and soon learned that booze like sex is a temporary fix, yet I got caught up in both. The vicious circle drove my misery index so high that there wasn't enough booze or pleasure to appease it. That's where I was the night Kirk brought you to the park.

"Seeing you again reminded me of everything I wanted and all I had lost. By that time I was convinced you would never forgive my fling with Emma. I had witnessed the pain David had caused you and he was repentant. I wasn't. I was angry and bitter.

"Confident the truth would rip you apart and you would dump me without looking back, I spewed it out with no hope of restoration."

Jesse had managed to stay in control of his words and emotions up to this point. He began to struggle. "Your forgiveness, Callie, was my undoing. I knew then that you loved me with a far greater love than I had known and certainly beyond anything I deserved. Your choice to forgive and that depth of love tore down all my defenses and silenced every excuse. I was speechless. My mind could not process forgiveness and love like that. My heart was afraid to believe it was true or possible. My inability to respond caused you to walk away.

"When you collapsed in Kirk's arms, I understood the cost of such love. All the doubts I'd ever had about your love for me vanished that night. I wanted to take you in my arms and thank you for loving me when I no longer loved myself, but Kirk was not going to allow me close to you again. I drove away broken ... confessing and forsaking my sins. Your love had won.

"Then Kirk started talking about you all the time. That threw me for a loop. I was jealous and I knew he was man enough and patient enough to win your heart if given time. I went home the next weekend and shared everything with my parents and Daniel, my former youth pastor. They agreed to hold me accountable but suggested that I needed help dealing with my feelings about David's part in your life. I contacted Joseph ... and here I am.

"My question is -- may I stay?" Jesse stood and leaned against the corner of her desk. "I was concerned about your answer until I took a trip to Bristol yesterday to mend fences and talk with an old friend. When I shared all that has happened since the three of us met at Lake Thunderbird, Kirk was confident that your answer would be yes. So with more confidence and hope than I've had since I left here last December, I ask again. Callie, is there still a place for me in your life?"

He moved beside her chair and knelt. He reached in his pocket and pulled out that little black ring box. Callie's heart could take no more. Before he could get another word out, she was hugging him and weeping out a definite, "YES!" Jesse stood and pulled her to her feet. As they embraced he whispered, "Will you marry me?" She nodded and lifted her finger. He gently slipped it on and lifted her chin. "I love you, Callie Girl."

"I love you, Cowboy."

The intensity of his ... their kiss ... put Callie on alert. "Excuse me, Mr. Collins, but we are going to have to set up some boundaries or get married soon. Which do you suggest?"

"I'd prefer marrying today, but will settle for late June. That gives you a little over three weeks. My thoughts are to make it a private family only deal. I did ask Kirk if he would be my best man and he agreed. I figured you'd want to see if Heather could make it. Then any time after the honeymoon, we can have a wedding reception and pull out all the stops. Joseph and our folks like this plan and are hoping you will come on board."

She backed away from him and put her hands on her hips. "How long has this coup been going on?"

He smiled. "Oh, it evolved as all of us began to talk about the possibilities. We're actually quite pleased with the package we are presenting to you. There's much wisdom in counsel and I've had much counsel ... so I figured this is mega wisdom. Back to my question. Think you can swing a June wedding? It works for my folks and yours. We are all waiting for your answer."

"Exactly how long have you been in town, Mr. Collins?" She looked ready to flog him.

"Easy, Sweetheart! I beat you by a day. I've been staying with Joseph and he made me promise to wait until today. All the other adults agreed with him and gave me the choices of being hogtied or cooperative. They threatened Carla with Alcatraz if she let it leak. I appeased her by asking her to be my spy after you arrived. I know what's been going on, Love of my life. Back to the question. Can you swing a June wedding?"

"Yes!" And she leaped into his arms.

Jesse kissed her again. "You wouldn't consider getting married any sooner, would you?"

"Three weeks will pass quickly, Jesse."

He grabbed her hand and hurried her down the hall to Joseph's office. Carla and her folks were already there talking to his folks on the phone.

"Callie, they are waiting for your answer."

Looking at the treasure before her with eyes that understood his worth, she responded with a grateful heart. "Yes, Jesse ... and his co-conspirators ... I think a June wedding is a lovely possibility."

And the plans to make the possibility a reality were set in motion.

# Chapter 46

The three weeks did pass quickly and tomorrow Jesse and Callie were getting married. He was getting ready to head back to the apartment they had rented when she asked him to sit in the porch swing with her for a while.

"Jesse, I'm going to share something very personal with you that I think you have the right to know."

"Please Callie, no more earth shattering surprises. Promise me. This porch holds some tough memories for me."

"I think I'm getting ready to erase all of those."

"Out with it, Callie Girl. Out with it! You are making me nervous. You're not calling off the wedding, are you?"

"You know better than that. I love you, Jesse Collins, and I'm eager to be your wife. And it's the wife part I want to talk about.

"I've been thinking about life and the roads we have traveled to get here. I recall that the thing that upset you the most on this porch was hearing of my second engagement to David. You spoke of always being number two in my life."

"I've come to terms with being your second number one man, Callie."

"Tonight I want to tell you about a place where you will always be number one, a place not even David has been."

She had his attention now. "Oh yeah. And where might that be?"

"I don't know if you ever wondered or figured it out, but you will be the first husband, the first man in my marriage bed. You, Jesse, not David."

His expression reminded her of a big kid on Christmas morning. "You mean …?"

"David taught me what unselfish love was and we shared that, but we never experienced that love expressed through a physical union. He married me to bless my future not to share the marriage bed. His injuries prevented that."

The impact of those words and that thought shook him to the core of his being. She was coming to him a virgin even though she had been married. He had wondered but dared not ask. He was going to be her number one husband in her marriage bed. Her number one lover. Wow!

Then sadness and grief broadsided him. Although he would be her number one lover, she would be his number two.

*She is marrying me knowing I have no such gift for her. God, the love this woman and David have demonstrated staggers me.*

He sat there in stunned amazement and disbelief and let the gift she would give to him tomorrow work through all those places and times he had questioned God in their relationship.

*I don't deserve this woman or her love any more than I deserve God or His love and yet both choose to love me. Both choose to forgive me. I choose to receive their love and I choose to live loving. I can do no less.*

He fell on his knees in front of her, grabbed her hands and asked her to forgive him for his jealously of David and his affair with Emma … though he had done so before. Somehow this confession involved a repentance that touched places the other had not … and something broke free in Jesse.

"Callie Henderson, soon to be Collins, from this day forward I want you to know that you can speak freely to me or anyone else about your love for and life with David with my blessings. I'll celebrate his birthday with you. I'll grieve with you on the anniversary of your marriage and his death.

"Today I can thank God for David and his impact on your life and mine … and ours.

"I'm about to come unglued here. I need to get home because I'm having married thoughts and I've got a few more hours to wait. I'll see you tomorrow afternoon, bride of mine."

He kissed her lightly and left.

*I may be the number two love of her life and even number two husband, but I'm going to be the number one husband in her bed — her number one lover.*

> *As a man to be married finds joy in his bride,*
> *so your God will find joy in you.*
> Isaiah 62:5b

# Epilogue
# Two Years later

Callie and Jesse did marry that June. Callie had worked full time with Joseph while Jesse finished his degree in business. His graduation was next week. Callie was five months pregnant but looked more like seven. She was ready to quit work and let Jesse take over her position.

Joseph had invited Jesse's family to stay with him for the celebration. After graduation, he provided a catered meal and hinted of special gifts for Jesse. When everyone had eaten their fill, he herded them into the den.

Callie had mentioned that she had a special graduation gift for Jesse, so Joseph got everyone's attention and nodded to Callie.

"Before I tell Jesse what his gift is, Uncle Joseph, we have a gift for you. You tell him, Jess."

Jesse grabbed her hand. "Callie and I have finally made a decision about the name of our baby. Joseph, if our baby is a boy, his name will be David Henderson Collins. If it's a girl, her name will be Ella Marie Collins."

The tears Joseph tried to hide rolled down his cheeks. He rose and hugged both. Several other folks were sniffling and wiping tears.

"What can I say ... but God bless you for your kindness."

He sat down and stray tears continued.

Callie pulled out a legal looking piece of paper and handed it to Jesse. "Jesse, these papers represent my forty percent shares in Henderson

Enterprises. Monday morning at 10:00 a.m. I will sign those over to you. You and Uncle Joseph will become partners."

Jesse remembered her making that promise before they married, but nothing else had ever been said. She loved him more than he could imagine, but he knew that she was learning from her number one Love, God. He stood and hugged her as much as a man can hug his very pregnant wife. "I love you, Callie Collins. Thank you for the trust that this gift entails. I won't let you, Joseph or David down." He sat down and was reaching to help her make a nest. She stopped him.

"Oh, yeah, there is something else." She placed her hands on her expanding middle. "Jesse, during my check-up yesterday, Dr. Barker advised me that we need to prepare for two babies instead of one. He heard two heartbeats which explains why I'm getting bigger faster than normal."

He stared at her and then her belly. "Twins?"

In fact at that moment all eyes in the room were staring at her protruding tummy. She nodded and held up two fingers. "Two!"

Margaret spoke up. "Jess, didn't you tell Callie about the twins in mine and your dad's families?"

He was still staring at Callie's baby container. "No, Mom. It never dawned on me that would happen to us."

Margaret laughed, "Callie, I have sisters who are twins and Dean has brothers who are twins. There is a good chance that any or all of our children will have twins."

With that announcement Jesse's siblings began to look at each other like they now had some contagious disease. All except Will. He looked at Carla and smiled.

Suddenly everyone got up and began to congratulate each other. Jesse pulled Callie into his arms. "Honey, is this okay with you? Can we handle twins?"

She laughed. "We can't send one back, Jesse, so I guess we'll learn to handle two. Besides, I've had twenty-four hours to adjust to the news and I'm excited. We'll do fine."

After everyone settled back down, Joseph indicated he had something to share. He reached into his coat pocket and pulled out a thick fold of paper and handed it to Jesse.

"What's this?" Jesse was still in shock over two babies instead of one ... and being a partner with Joseph.

"Ella and I had this place built with a large family in mind. She had one miscarriage before David and two afterwards. A hysterectomy followed that and our hopes were dashed. About a week before his accident, David told me that he was hopeful that our dream of filling this house with children was just around the corner.

"Monday at 9 a.m. the three of us have an appointment to meet with our lawyer. He will see that this deed is transferred to your names. From the day you two told me of your pregnancy and your desire to have a large family, I realized it was the daughter of my heart and my partner who would fulfill the Henderson dream and fill this house.

"I have kept five acres at the edge of the property where construction will begin on a smaller version of this home next week. I'll rent an apartment if the house isn't finished before the babies come.

"We have to get you moved in before too long. Callie's probably past moving now. I will be taking very little furniture when I leave. Most of what's here is yours, if you want it.

"Not only did David love you, Callie. Ella loved you. Both would want me to do this.

"I only have one request. Fill it. This house has begged for a large family for years. At the rate you're going, it won't take long."

Now Callie and Jesse were in shock. Their parents weren't fairing any better. Jesse's brothers and Lizzie were already planning to visit the Ponderosa, especially Will.

True to form, Carla spoke up first. "Well, David can fill one room and Ella another. That only leaves three more. Any triplets in either family? Or you could have two or three more sets of twins and just double up in the five bedrooms. You could easily house ten kids here."

With that thought, Callie and Jesse sat down, while pandemonium replaced all decorum as folks let the possibility of those thoughts dominate the conversations.

After the Oklahoma crowd headed home, the Virginia folks shifted gears trying to prepare for their double blessings.

Jesse was excited about work. Callie was more than ready to stay home. She was put on bed rest her last six weeks and three weeks before her due date, David and Ella were born. Carla had been right!

While Callie was in the hospital, her family and friends moved the Jesse Collins family into the place Callie had once described as next door to Eden.

As he was driving his new family home, Jesse stopped at the entrance. He had put up a new sign. *The Collins Clan of Henderson Hills*. Callie was pleased, "Thank you, Jesse."

Callie looked at the two treasures in her arms. Precious little Ella had her dark features, while David was a carbon copy of Jesse. How like God! Though this earthly family was definitely the product of love's union between her and her precious number two yet number one husband, Jesse, she knew in her heart that it was also the spiritual offspring of her number one husband, David and his unselfish love.

*Love never comes to an end!!*

Dear Reader,

Thank you for joining Callie, David and Jesse as they each search for the answer to the universal cry of every heart. I pray that their journey connected with yours at times.

I trust that somewhere along the way, your spirit identified with God's desire for a personal, intimate relationship with you, and that by the last page you were fully convinced that you are pursued, loved and treasured by the God who formed you in your mother's womb.

The *Treasured* pen story is an adaptation of an actual event in my own life while writing this book. I found the pen in a parking lot the day I was shopping for the treasures to go in Callie's trunk for the cover shoot. It was my granddaughter who brought my attention to the gift I had found. It was a dear cousin's research skills that identified the manufacturer and retail information. The response was my own.

Never doubt that you are loved and treasured.

JB Price

If you have questions or comments, you may contact me at
[pricejb490@gmail.com](mailto:pricejb490@gmail.com)

# Acknowledgements

I am forever grateful to our Heavenly Father whose love birthed the story. Your love has won my heart!

A grateful thank you to Christian Hidalgo and Navigation Advertising for the attractive cover. I'm impressed by your talent and honored to call you son-in-law.

Thank you, Barbara Moffett, talented cousin and dear friend, for gently pushing me out of my comfort zone. Among the voices that encouraged me to write, yours stands out.

A heartfelt thanks to my prayer partners and special friends, Jayne Turner and Lisa Bowker, who have walked with me through every step of this adventure. You are treasures.

Multiplied thanks to my book buddies, Laura Brown, Barbara Hargis, Joyce Reed, Angi Rudder, Pat Darrell, Linda Sykes, Sarah Barnes, and Lokelani Tangaro for listening for hours with your hearts to mine. Many of your shared insights have been woven into the fabric of this story.

A group thanks to the ladies of the 2013 fall retreat. Storytelling took on a new dimension for me that weekend. Your responses encouraged me to share Callie's story with others. Hope you like the changes that your thoughts inspired.

A life time of thanks to my ninety-two year old Mom who taught me to love and treasure God's Word, and to my sister, Connie, whose sense of humor and gift for gab has made her the favorite family storyteller.

Rachel and Jennifer, having you and your families in my life has given me a clearer understanding of the heart of God for us, His children. Never doubt that you are loved and treasured -- imperfectly by me -- but perfectly by the One who formed you in the womb and set eternity in your hearts.

And Barry, husband of many years, I searched the dictionary trying to find the words to describe the love you have demonstrated day in and day out. I've decided unselfish and unconditional say it best. It has been your love that has given me insight into the love of Christ for His bride. You are a dearly held treasure … by Him and me.

# About the Author

JB Price earned an undergraduate degree from Carson Newman College and a master's degree from Middle Tennessee State University. She has been a public school teacher, a home school educator focusing on autism, dyslexia, and ADHD and a friend to women in crisis for thirty-plus years. Growing up in the hills of East Tennessee in a culture rich in storytelling and having a dad who loved to spin a tale led to a fascination for appealing yarns and engaging stories at an early age. Writing snippets for family and friends and using stories to teach became second nature. Writing a book, however, had never been a dream or consideration. Thus, the birth of this book was quite unexpected.

JB was scheduled to lead a retreat in the fall of 2013 with the theme of love and intimacy. While she struggled with an effective way to not only teach but also engage the hearts of the ladies, a plot began to unfold. This book resulted. God has used the story and the work involved in writing and publishing to teach and engage the writer's own heart regarding God's love and desire for intimacy.

JB and her husband live on a small farm on the outskirts of Murfreesboro, Tennessee.